DRACULA BEYOND STOKER

Issue 7

DBS Press

Dracula Beyond Stoker
Issue 7

Tucker Christine
editor

Edward G. Pettit
Shannon Vare Christine
consulting editors

Published by DBS Press
ISBN - 978-1-963391-12-1 (Paperback)
ISBN - 978-1-963391-13-8 (e-book)
November, 2025

www.dbspress.com
www.draculabeyondstoker.com

Contents

Letter, Editor to the Reader

31 October

My dearest reader,—

It should come as no surprise that Mina would anchor a strong issue—she is arguably the most resilient character in *Dracula*, the keeper of the secrets (and the manuscript), and the heart and soul of the Crew of Light. The stories you're about to read expand upon her strength and resolve, while also depicting a woman who is haunted but never broken.

Tyler Kitchenman opens the issue at the end of the novel, with Mina uncovering a secret hidden in a crypt at the edge of Dracula's castle. Mark Oxbrow's "I Shall Not Fear" puts her in a race against time to save her granddaughter, while Vince Stadon presents a Mina who takes a radically different path than readers might expect. In Henry Herz's "Alliance of Convenience," Renfield and Dracula finally meet Mina—with dire consequences.

Bill Cozza, R.S. Tiemstra, Dennis K. Crosby, and Macoy Greco each offer us visions of Mina as adventurer and monster hunter, while the inimitable Doris V. Sutherland crafts a tale of reincarnation and gender politics.

In Lindy Ryan's "The Harrow Letters," a Mina who has lived longer than she imagined awaits the end, while Gwendolyn Kiste's "A Mina for All Seasons" allows our heroine to relive the same events across multiple lives and timelines.

As always, we resurrect a classic: Cynthia Ward's "Whoever Fights Monsters." And to close, James S. Dorr offers a haunting final note with his poem, "Chagrin du Vampire."

Taken together, these pieces remind us that Mina is never just one thing—never only a victim, never merely a witness. She is enduring, adaptable, and central to *Dracula*'s legacy. Now, turn the page and join Mina Harker on these journeys—through time, across lives, and into the heart of horror itself.

Enjoy,

Tucker

The Flowerless Tomb
By Tyler Kitchenman

Death settled around her. It was rooted deep, a gnarled tree stubbornly clinging to this world. The forest was still and quiet. Faint footfalls, paws penetrating deep within the snow, avoiding the largest of the forest's debris, provided only a muffled crunch. Still, beasts encircled the woman. Only then, after her mind could no longer stave off what her senses implored upon her, that something was coming, did she wake completely.

Mina's eyes rose above the tree line searching for an absent sun. The air hung still. Grey skies seemed to press down upon her. The air suddenly, aggressively pulled itself through her. The frigid Transylvanian winter was unforgiving. Snow littered the landscape, leaving the vista bleached with ice. The clearing sat muddied and gray after countless animals had trod the permafrost. How long had she been here? They had been traveling for days, with only death and despair behind them. There was no telling where Jonathan and the others were. The good doctor had left hours ago, or minutes? How long had she lain there amongst the trees? Mina tried to remember what had transpired the night before. The brides had descended upon them. Doctor Van Helsing staved them off; he held the beasts at bay. But then…where had he gone? Mina's mind sloshed loosely within her skull. Hypnosis, one of the doctor's many tricks, could only work for so long. And here, in this cursed place, she didn't expect notions of science and reason to hold much weight against something far older and darker. If this truly were the time of enlightenment, as Doctor Van Helsing claimed it was, then he'd come to the darkest place on the face of the earth with a torch. Mina only hoped it would burn bright enough.

There was no life left in London. Not with the Count still alive? Jonathan would not say such a thing, but Mina knew it. Lucy was gone. These men—these soldiers—they'd given so much already. London was blood. Their collective past stood now sullied and stained lest they remove this beast from the world. That is what they should call him, the beast. Dracula was the devil, and now that Mina stood in this abyssal landscape, a forest of cold and death, she felt closer to him, closer than ever before.

Mina knew the doctor had left her for good reason. Despite the uncertainties that floated through her foggy mind, she knew Abraham would not abandon her. He'd gone on to the castle. To prevent the Count's return. Mina could feel the hate bubble up from her stomach. None of the others could possibly understand. Within her, two hearts twisted themselves up, muscles tearing and tangling into one. Mina's love for her friends—for Jonathan —and her humanity resided deep within her chest. But alongside her true heart, nestled there in the darkness of her flesh, beat a darker, more vengeful heart. There, her love for the Count, or rather, his pull on her, littered her chest with the grotesque rhythm of a love so wretchedly lost. She knew those feelings, as genuine as they were, were not her own. She stifled the bile and pushed the thoughts of the doctor from her mind.

The plan was simple and already in motion. With Van Helsing gone, there was no hope of further hypnosis to help resist the draw of the Count. She'd have to manage on her own. But as the distance between any actor in this quest and herself increased, Mina felt the hateful urges subside. With none around her so bent on the Count's destruction, she found it easier to push the thoughts of sabotage from her mind. In their place remained a dull yearning, a pull to the castle, to her home.

Mina shuddered. She only needed to endure. A distant *crack* sounded in the fading light. Scurrying footfalls sprayed snow out across the corners of Mina's vision. They were surrounding her, the creatures of the night. The music of the dark forest, suddenly so loud, reminded Mina that she was not alone. She needed to move, to find a point of defense. There, in the clearing, she was far too vulnerable.

Frail and alone, Mina Harker pulled herself to her feet. The border of the ring was apparent on the ground around her. But she knew that to the natural beasts of the forest, the doctor's work provided no protection. Mina reached down and grasped a smoldering torch from the remains of the fire. She caressed its tip and hushed a warm breath of life into the embers. The torch bore a sudden burst of flame into the winter air. Just as a howl broke— so close that the steam of the predator's breath rose like a vaporous specter at the border of the clearing—Mina broke into a mad dash.

Her leather boots thudded on the frozen ground beneath her, and the sound was unmistakably foreign when joined by the clattering patter of paws behind her. Mina could feel the trees swallow her whole as the light faded all around her. The safety of the clearing, although short-lived with the wolves fast approaching, suddenly felt like a cherished memory. They were gaining on her.

Did her master know that she ran for her life? Could he protect her here? Could he command those subject to his will even while he slept? Loyal thoughts and inclinations oozed through her skull. The Count's hold was still upon her. She ran not just from the wolves and all manner of beasts, she ran from the Count, she ran from London, she ran from death itself.

The setting sun spewed cascades of fractured light across the forest floor. Mina ran through the sun's many fingers, feeling their pull of warmth. She needed to find something to provide her with an equal footing, something to put her back against. She could swing the torch, perhaps stave off the attack until the good doctor found her. The idea presented itself as logic; it provided momentary comfort. But Mina knew she'd stand little chance against a pack of ravenous wolves. She began to weave through the trees. A low-hanging branch tore at her shoulder. She spun momentarily, catching a glimpse of the horde trailing her. Flashes of ivory-white teeth, yellow eyes, and mangey fur, the color of gun smoke, danced behind her. She regained her footing and lurched forward. Suddenly, the ground fell out from beneath her feet. A steep embankment gave way to a sloping hill. Mina landed hard on her side and began to tumble down the incline toward a narrow gulch at the base of a small forest valley. The sky slid in and out of view. With each roll, Mina's shoulder, and then her ribs, and finally her head, met the earth. And then, with an impact like wet hide against stone, she was still. For a moment, a sheet of whiteness filled her vision. A dull brownish haze replaced the light until she found her focus. She could see the beasts pacing atop the edge of the embankment. They seemed to hesitate for some reason. A larger wolf, a shock of black fur ridged against his spine, tracing down to his tail, howled into the twilight. Mina imagined this beast was the leader of the pack. She'd remember it.

She pulled herself to her knees. Blindly, she fumbled through the decaying foliage around her, feeling her way. She needed to keep her eyes aloft. She met the alpha's gaze. In her heart, deep, somewhere deeper than what it means to be human, she knew that if she broke his gaze, he'd come for her. Her fingers finally grasped the torch once again. She lifted the end of the stout spear ahead of her only to confirm what she already knew. The fall extinguished the flame.

It didn't matter. The doctor would be looking for her by now. She could use the torch as a weapon. She'd club the beast to death. A fervor rose in her chest, one she'd never known before. She was ready. She would meet them as equals. And then, suddenly, a wolf standing at the back of the pack spat a short yelp into the chilling air.

The alpha's gaze rose above Mina and seemed to register something behind her. She'd never seen such emotion in an animal's eyes. But at that moment, the wolf comprehended whatever was standing behind her; she could see it. The wolf's glare, his entire demeanor, shifted to one of passivity. As quickly as they had descended upon her, the wolves were gone.

Slowly, prepared for some manner of creature not yet known to her imagination, Mina turned around to meet her undesired savior. There before her stood a dilapidated stone structure no more than a meter or so across with a slanted stone gable; the crumbling structure appeared morbidly solemn, a crypt of sorts. Mina swayed on her feet. Here, at the bottom of a gulch along the North side of the castle, the building sat alone without any sense of ceremony or adornment. It was a tomb, a final resting place that none seemed to have visited in some time. And, just as the full comprehension of the structure coalesced in her mind, Mina registered two things almost simultaneously: the tomb's door was ajar, and from the threshold a pale, decrepit hand slid from sight, its skeletal fingers rasping against the disintegrating stone.

Her heart leapt into her throat. Despite the fear brought on by the wolves and other beasts of the forest, Mina had resolved to feel alone, as if she were the only creature capable of design within these trees. Here, she was no longer alone. Her finger pressed into the warming wood, cutting the circulation in her hand, cracking the knuckles. Her fingers were as white as the demon she'd just witnessed. Another howl split the air of the coming night. The pack was clearly cautious of this place, but they were reluctant to abandon a meal that so willingly wandered into their den. She could make out the outline of several figures on her flanks. The wolves would try again. She needed to make a decision, and fast. She thought of something her father had always said. How can we use our enemies in a time of dire need?

"We make them our friends." She hissed in a hushed whisper. And then she plunged herself into the darkness before her, allowing the tomb to swallow her whole.

A structure standing that close to the castle could hardly be a coincidence. What need did the Count have for such a clandestine resting place? Although it did not feel secret. As Mina stumbled through the darkness, feeling her way for some sense of orientation, her mind drifted to another feeling: abandonment.

The Count had built this tomb here in the shadow of the castle, not to mourn the dead, but to forget them.

A metallic clang echoed in the hollow chamber. Mina could no longer stifle her screams. She cut the silence that followed the ringing of the tomb's metal gate with a sudden cry of fear.

"Your mind does not deceive you. I am the forgotten." The voice was winter wind dragging its claws through infertile soil. Mina could see within the sound a choked whisper hissing out from the decaying cavity of an arid throat. She froze, a statue to finally adorn the barren crypt.

"Do not fear me, child. I will not harm you, not here." The voice was all around her. She could not place its origin. But as this entity continued to speak, it resolved itself into something akin to a human. Courage found her along with a rancid memory.

"I am no child to you nor friend. And you are not the first to call me this." Her voice was sharp and true, striking like a defining stroke of a sword.

There was only silence. No breath but her own graced the air.

And then, it spoke again.

"Yes. I know. And now, you've come all this way to what? Kill him?"

This thing knew. How could this be? She imagined this dying thing in league with the Count. It was the most logical deduction. It was perhaps the undead alliance they had all feared. What could she do?

"Above you. Look up. Use the torch to pull those vines free. It will bring you peace, my…friend. And then, we will talk." The being's whisper found tone and now, with it, age. Despite the timeless quality of the entity's patience, the voice sounded young, perhaps even younger than her own.

Hesitantly, Mina looked up. Above her, cut into the ceiling of the tomb's interior, a circular opening bore into the stone. The remnant of a long-forgotten skylight, now overtaken by vines and dead growth. Without a thought, Mina plunged the torch upward, a twisted semblance of King Arthur after pulling the sword from the stone flashed across her mind. She swung and tore the torch through the frail and splintering branches and vines until they began to fall free of the opening. With a final ripping swing, the vines gave way to a pouring bloom of fading sunlight. The valley suddenly seemed perfectly positioned for maximum light to find the opening. Even at the dying hour of twilight, a beam fell upon the tomb's floor, encapsulating Mina in its glow.

Mina began to understand. She looked back into the darkness, and even though her eyes provided no truth, she knew he was standing before her. Slowly, like the eyes of a serpent rising from black waters, two hands slid into view. Mina could immediately see the aging silver manacles clasped around each wrist. And then, the hands and forearms began to smoke in the light.

"Even if I could overcome my chains. The light keeps you safe." And just as the creature's skin seemed to sizzle like fresh meat dripping with scalding fat, the demonstration was over.

Mina waited. She could sense something akin to Jonathan's negotiations at work. He'd often come home late and recount the daily trials of the office over a brandy. Mina was keenly aware that she was participating in a power struggle. This thing wanted to see where she stood, as it were. Could she reckon with another member of the undead?

"It is true. I am undead." The creature spoke again, from all around her.

Her throat caught. She had suspected it, but she also knew fear was a corrupting force. But the idea lingered far longer this time, refusing to dissipate. This creature could read her mind. And just as she thought this…

"Yes. That is also true. In a manner of speaking, I suppose." There was a slight lilt in his voice this time. It was as if she could hear the creature's grin as he said this. He? She supposed from what she knew of the Count that she would need to accept that this creature, too, once held humanity.

"I know what you are thinking. I do not need to see it, or, how do you say? Read it. I simply know it. So, it is best for us to be honest with one another, yes?"

"You are a vampire. A creature of the night. A Nosferatu." She spoke firmly, but was unable to conceal the tremble in her voice in the end. From the depths of the tomb, a scratching rasp whirred up around her. Mina was at first unsure what the sound was, and only after the sound resolved itself into a mucousy tumult did she understand that the creature was laughing.

"I am many things. They never cease to conjure a new moniker as the decades slip by. What concern is this of mine? None. It matters not. I am cursed. It is that simple."

Mina found her strength. She straightened her back, only then realizing she had been appropriating the shape of a question mark. The creature chortled mockingly.

"You *are* cursed. A monster. You must murder to live."

Just as the words left her lips, the carcass slopped across the stone floor into the fading light. It sounded like a sack of rotting vegetables. The hare's emaciated body lay strewn at Mina's feet. She shuddered at the sight.

"I kill whenever an unlucky beast wanders into my cell. Otherwise, I starve."

Mina stared at the hare. There was no blood, not a single trace of crimson. And as she spoke, she held her gaze on the dead animal.

"And if not, you die?" She wasn't sure if she had thought it or said it aloud. But of course, it did not matter.

"No, young. I starve."

"For how long?"

Mina knew already what awaited her gaze. The sun, now performing its final cresting dive behind the horizon, angled the light perfectly into the tomb, casting a glancing glow out beyond the border of the circle. She knew he was standing there, and if she looked up, she would see him. He wanted her to look up. She could feel it on her skin. Her flesh seemed to coil and raise, extending the small hairs along her flesh erect as if he was pulling her towards him.

"Forever." He spoke.

Mina looked up. Before her stood a tall figure with square shoulders and a cold set of blue eyes. His robes were tattered, his scalp bare, and he was unmistakably dead. The creature's skin held no moisture whatsoever. It clung to him like warped leather. His chin was blackened, stained obsidian from the years of life drained from the small, helpless creatures of the forest. A few stray hairs, as pale as the moon, clung to the outer edges of his skull. Despite the sound of his voice, which Mina admitted to herself to be congenial and warm, even inviting, the creature was visibly weak; too weak to be of any threat.

"What do I call you?" Mina never once faltered, even in the face of such endless suffering. She knew too much. She understood.

"You do not call me Dracula. Of that much, you can be certain." He held her gaze, seemingly impressed with her resolve. It was as if he had expected her to run from the tomb screaming. Which, of course, every fiber of her body had demanded. But she hadn't. As he spoke, he turned to pace as far as the chains would allow. Old habits died hard, she supposed. He would walk around this woman like a leviathan circling its prey.

"I am the first. I am made in his image. I was here long before he made those playthings up in his castle. For this, I think you will call me, Adam."

Mina laughed. He amused her, she had to admit it. Back in London, when the Count had come for her, part of her had wanted it. She'd never admit the full scale of those emotions to Jonathan. She would take the sensation to her grave. But as this creature spoke, she felt something similar. It wasn't a feeling of desire. But all the same, she knew that she was safe. This thing did not wish her any harm.

"You hold disdain for the brides?" Mina adjusted her footing.

The creature let out a resounding cackle. "Brides! No, I say playthings. I have no respect for these ornaments. It is tragic for some time. But this is why he keeps them. They…accommodate his will. You understand?" As the creature spoke, shuffling across the room like a crone, it produced a small wooden stool from the corner. It placed the stool just at the edge of the light. After a moment's pause, Mina took it and sat upon the stool, positioning it at the center of the soft fading light.

"Yes, be comfortable, please," Adam said.

Mina found herself astounded. This poor thing, it wanted to speak with her. It wanted her to know these things, hear these things. It probably hadn't spoken in years, perhaps decades. And then, she thought that too.

"No, he comes to me. He speaks to me. But I stopped answering long ago." The creature sat down upon the cool stone floor. He looked up at her with a waning smile.

"You do not wish to speak with him?" She asked.

The creature—or rather, Adam—held his smile, soft and inviting. It was as if no matter how emaciated these creatures would become, they would always retain their attraction, that predatory pull that they willed upon all those around them.

"Tell me, child. Why do you come to this place?" He asked.

"You know why I've come," Mina said plainly.

His smile faded.

"You have come to do what many have already tried and failed."

"I won't fail." Her jaw clenched, and her fingers curled. She spoke this as if she spoke it into existence.

"No, here, I suspect you will not. I can sense that. I can feel what burns inside of you, the depth of your rage. It is like a need, no? But do you want to ensure that you truly succeed?" The creature bowed its head. The movement further concealed the monster's countenance within the shadows.

"Of what do you speak?" She implored him.

"I was the first. And if you succeed, your dear Lucy will be the last."

Mina's heart tightened within her chest at the mention of her friend's name.

"And?" She demanded, trembling as she beckoned the creature to continue.

"There are more," he said.

She understood what he was saying, but for some reason, the idea failed to take hold. Her mind could not grasp the horror he had suggested. Abraham would kill the brides; that was his plan, and she trusted that he would see it through. They, all of them, would kill Dracula. And then, only then, would this nightmare fade away. It must be so.

"Don't forget me, my child."

"You are the child. Spare me your placation. I know what you are." A fire blazed in her chest that surprised her. She had no idea that ferocity was there, that it lurked within her. Who was this creature to reject everything they had planned, everything they had worked so hard for? She would end this, and this creature, this boy, really, made no difference to the matter. Only then did Mina truly see the being that once was, the man before the beast. And it was true—the word *man* served the mortal structure of this being no truth. Whenever this creature had been human, he would have been far younger than even Mina herself. This vampire was once a young boy. The thought struck Mina with a sudden melancholy that stifled her rage, extinguishing her fury.

"You plan to kill my father. This I know. I implore you, do so. Post haste. Do not avail. But know this. He is not the end of this, nor am I. My father was careless with his seed before nature saw fit to curse him for eternity, and his recklessness knew no bounds afterward. The frivolity with which he embraced his curse, his plague, bordered on insanity."

The creature paced rapidly. He spewed the information as if it streamed forth from a long-clogged geyser, pressure building over time. He needed to share it. It gave him purpose.

"They will die as he does. When he is slain, they will cease to be." Mina spoke this timidly, softly, as if she only uttered it as a wish. Which, of course, she knew was all it was.

"We are too old. We have too long been in league with the night. We are our own and must be slain accordingly." With this, the creature quickly spun in place and hastened across the tomb toward a small alcove formed in the back wall of the structure. There, he lit a candle, illuminating a large bronze shield adorned with the indentation of a dragon. The beast rose its massive, fanged jaws above a snow-peaked mountain and spewed flames from its jaws. Above the shield hung a large sword rusted with age. Adam paused at the altar. He reached, stretching his hands out beneath the shield, and pulled free a small wooden box. Inside, resting amongst dry hay and other remnants of the forest floor, lay a tiny doll with golden hair. Adam's gangling fingers caressed the figure.

"Even I have memory. Even I had love. In my heart, I know it to be true. That is our true curse."

Mina understood. She was inheriting knowledge that could potentially lead to the end of the vampire forever.

"No. It is not mere knowledge. It is a secret. You must keep this with you. To know they exist is to know their weakness. You are already a threat to my kind with as much as you know now." He spoke with his back still turned to her, with the doll still held loftily in his hands.

"There are others like you? Others who can hear my thoughts?"

"There are those who have had practice, just as I have." Adam thrust his arms upward and detached the sword from the stone wall, ripping it downward, sending small bits of crumbling stone out around him in a hissing spray. He swept back across the tomb, moving like the surge of a winter wind preceding a tempest. He offered her the sword. Without hesitation, she accepted it. The cool iron was heavy in her arms. Her grip barely covered the handle beneath the hilt. She could feel the weight in her bones, how she could use it to her advantage.

"With this blade, you accept the responsibility I bestow upon you. Hunt them down, destroy them. Rid this world of the vampire, Mina Harker." As he said this, Adam knelt at Mina's feet and bowed his head, allowing the tip of his greying skull to kiss the fading sunlight. Just as Adam's skin began to smolder, Mina lifted the sword.

I t was black. It ran from the stump slowly, viscous, like an ooze of the earth, something lost to time. As the boy's blood pooled at Mina's feet, she could feel the end creeping up behind her. She turned, paying no mind to the head that had rolled off into the darkness, and walked from the tomb.

There, standing just outside the tomb, she knew two things: she would never tell the others about Adam—her heart could hardly bear the weight alone, why spread that plague of memory to those she loved—and her life would never be the same. She would hunt the vampires to extinction.

Mina Harker stood there in the forest's growing silence and exhaled a wafting plume of warm breath into the still air. And then, from behind her, she could hear Doctor Van Helsing calling out her name. She dropped the sword, allowing the weight of its past to plunge it deep into the frozen, blood-stained ground. She turned and hurried off in the direction of her name, gathering her resolve. Night was almost upon them. Confidently, Mina left Adam's body behind as she raced toward the castle to kill the boy's father.

Tyler Kitchenman is a teacher and writer in Bucks County, Pennsylvania. He teaches creative writing, English composition, and theater arts at Quakertown Senior High School. He also manages the theater program and directs the shows. Tyler has earned a bachelor's degree in English Literature with a focus on creative writing and a Bachelor's degree in filmmaking with a focus on screenwriting, both from Temple University. He has earned a Master's of Liberal Arts from the University of Pennsylvania. Tyler self-published a collection of short works available on Amazon's Kindle. He has also completed several short pieces of fiction, a few plays, and has multiple manuscripts underway, in addition to a completed novel.

I Shall Not Fear
By Mark Oxbrow

MINA HARKER'S JOURNAL

2 November 1922.—For Séraphine.

One day, beloved, when I am gone, you will read these words and know the truth.

I was a school mistress, such an innocent. Twenty-one years old, teaching young ladies the finer points of etiquette.

It should have been an unforgettable year. An endless, blissful summer of weddings and honeymoons. My dearest friend in all the world was to be married. Lucy Westenra. I named your aunt Lucy in her memory. Lucy was fearless.

She was nineteen. We ate vanilla cake, dancing and drinking glasses of champagne at her birthday. We thought that there was nothing to fear in all the world. We would love and live forever.

Lucy would be Lady Godalming, and I would be her principal bridesmaid.

We talked of a thousand things that seemed so important. What charms we would hide in the tiers of the wedding cake. The list of guests: friends and relatives with their odd quirks and family secrets. We wondered in hushed tones if it might be better to elope. We shared the names we hoped to call our children.

Your grandfather Jonathan courted me most earnestly. He brought me posies of spring flowers and mumbled desperately, tripping over his words as we took walks in the park. Never had I met such a bumbling and adorable gentleman. I was besotted.

I was determined to be an industrious and devoted wife.

Jonathan's work took him to Transylvania before we could marry. I dreamed of a June wedding. Long hazy summer days. Hay in the fields. Bumblebees and butterflies. Jonathan set sail in April. A matter of weeks, he said, no more. Some legal papers to deliver by hand. A Transylvanian aristocrat, Dracula, was buying a number of properties in London. He wanted to read over the particulars before signing.

May dawned, and I remember chimney sweeps and milkmaids dancing out in the streets. They raised a maypole, tied with bright ribbons and garlanded with flowers and oak leaves. I counted the days until Jonathan's return. The May days died, and I sat alone as June inched toward July. No wedding bells. No letters. Nothing but fear knotting in the pit of my stomach.

A letter. It arrived on August 19th. Jonathan was convalescing at the Hospital of St Joseph and St Mary, in Buda-Pesth. He was delirious, raving of wolves and poison, monsters and blood. I travelled at once, to be with him and nurse him. We were married at his bedside. Such a sombre wedding, a thousand miles from England and everyone we loved.

Séraphine, you will know by now of Dracula. Of his dreadful voyage to England on the Demeter. The shipwreck at Whitby. You will know that vampires are not fanciful things. They are flesh and blood, deathless.

Dracula took Lucy's life.

He took everything from her. Every moment of joy she should have felt. The love that was her due. The sound of her children's laughter. Dracula murdered her.

Doubtless you have read Mr. Stoker's book. He took on the daunting task of compiling our letters, diary pages and wax cylinder recordings to piece together our remembrances of that year. I cannot fault him. He has brought to light all that was fit to publish. Some forty pages or so were cut from his original draft. No publisher of sound mind would print such horrors.

With Lucy gone, we hunted Dracula.

We traced boxes of earth from Transylvania to England. Destroying them, one by one, denying him any refuge. And in his rage, Dracula turned his wrath on me.

As I write these words, I can taste his blood in my mouth. I will never forget. Dracula fed on me. Tightened his hand about my throat. I saw his fingers curl into a fist, felt him strike me across the face. He hit me with the back of his hand, the blow splitting the skin across my forehead, cutting my lips open on my teeth. Blood ran into my eyes.

He raised me high, off my feet, as I choked and fought to breathe.

And he smiled. Above all, I wish I could unsee that smile. He tore a ragged hole in his chest and smeared his dead blood in my face. Fetid, decaying blood. Putrefied. Rust and mould. Thick and black as treacle.

He left me, broken and bloodied. I have never known such fear.

In his arrogance, Dracula never imagined that we could defeat him. He left me there to die. To turn, and to kill and feast. I would be his revenge on them all. Jonathan and Van Helsing, Arthur, Seward, Quincey. They would be forced to watch me die. There was nothing they could do to save me. Nothing but cut off my head and burn my body.

I felt it then. When I woke and stared at my bruised and broken face. John Seward had stitched my cuts and tended my wounds. Lines of neat doctor's stitches ran from my left eye to my scalp. I still bear the scars.

Seward held a light up to my face, to see the pupils dilate in my eyes. I felt him close. Listened as the air rushed into his lungs. Heard his heart beating. The pulse of the blood under his skin. I wanted to feed on him. I desired blood. Craved it.

I wanted to rip out Jonathan's throat. It was rapturous. Intoxicating.

This was the purest bliss. To feast. To devour human flesh like a Bacchante. Fingers dripping red with blood. Tearing meat with my teeth. I never knew such a yearning.

I do not know how I held back. The desire was overwhelming. I knew if I succumbed, I would be lost. Damned.

Dracula's dead blood ran in my veins, swirling in my heart. Corrupting me. But I saw things. Saw with his eyes. We hunted him. Raced headlong to Transylvania. To his castle.

I never knew the names of Dracula's weird sisters. Van Helsing went alone into the catacombs to face them. I lay, knees clutched to my chest, vomiting black bile, within a circle of Sacred Wafers. But now I know their names. Izabela Lupu. Lacramioara Fieraru. Sofia Lazarescu. The Professor hammered wooden stakes into their hearts and hacked off their heads. Dracula's three vampire brides.

The sun was dying behind the mountains as Dracula and his Szgany breached the gate, with Jonathan and Quincey, Arthur and Seward, fearless, at their heels. It was butcher's work. Guns and knives. Bodies falling. Bullets digging into flesh.

I saw a Szgany blade plunged deep into Quincey's body. God forgive me. I wanted to tear at the wound with my bare hands. To feed on him, smothering my face in his warm blood.

And in that moment, I saw Dracula.

Quincey lunged, his bowie knife piercing Dracula's chest, buried deep in his dead heart. Jonathan's Kukri knife slashed across Dracula's throat.

I fell to my knees, looking down at my hands. They were trembling. I was hexed, spellbound like a girl in a fairy tale, but now the curse was raised. I was Mina. I could breathe. I was free.

It took years for us to heal. Arthur was married, as was Doctor Seward. Van Helsing took his leave, returning to Amsterdam. Seven years later, Jonathan and I travelled to Transylvania with our young son, Quincey—your father. Named for the courageous Quincey Morris, who gave his life that I might live.

As a boy, your father was always a dreamer. Quincey loved stories and books of adventure. He would read Treasure Island over and over until the spine split and the pages fell out.

And then we were blessed with a daughter, your aunt Lucy. She was wild from the first, scrabbling about in puddles and smearing mud on her best dresses. She made potions with bits of dead flowers, rainwater and mouldy leaves.

We had another daughter, Beatrice. We lost her before you were born. She was such a happy child. She was taken by the Spanish Flu three years ago. I would have died in her place. Without a second thought. My children are more precious to me than life itself.

I always feared that the dark was not done with us.

Dracula was gone but the veil had fallen from my eyes. Monsters, the un-dead, all of it is real. The things that children fear. Vampires, boggarts, hobgoblins and werewolves. Dreadful things with teeth and claws.

I hoped we would be spared, but I swore I would be prepared.

Arthur, Lord Godalming, taught me how to shoot. I had barely seen a gun when I was first handed a revolver. Arthur took Jonathan and I to Scotland, to his Highland estate, where his ghillie took us grouse shooting and stalking deer. We learned to shoot with rifles, shotguns, pistols and revolvers.

In London I learned to fight with blades. I sought out Captain Alfred Hutton and Egerton Castle as my tutors. I mastered the sabre, rapier and buckler. Hutton led a revival in historical duelling for the stage, teaching actors in London's theatres how to fight with sword and dagger. I saw *Romeo and Juliet* at the Lyceum in 1908, keenly following each lunge and parry the actors made.

I shared what I learned of cane fighting with my friend Kitty Marshall. Kitty was one of Emmeline Pankhurst's bodyguards, keeping her out of the hands of the police as they played 'cat and mouse' with the suffragettes. Kitty was taught ju-jitsu by Edith Garrud. She did her best to teach me, but I admit that I was a poor student.

Millions were slain in the Great War. Your father Quincey fought at Mons, at the Somme and at Passchendaele. He lost so many dear friends but by God's grace he was spared.

Quincey met your mother Élise a year after the war's end. They married in Paris. Their wedding would be the last time my beloved children were together. Quincey and Élise began their lives in the 11th arrondissement. Lucy returned to Scotland, to her medical studies at the University of Edinburgh. Jonathan and I took Beatrice back to London. She died three months later.

Séraphine—your mother and father have chosen such a beautiful name for you.

My granddaughter. To bundle you up and hold you. So small, and warm and soft. Fragile.

I should have known the dark would come for us. At that moment of happiness, when you were a helpless, innocent baby. When all seemed safe and healed.

I did not know her when she welcomed us at the Galeries Lafayette. The vampire. How did I not sense it? It is unforgivable. Ana Mathilde Helena Floris she called herself. A lie. 'Meister Harker' she said, smiling. 'There is something so familiar about your face.'

I was a fool. She gave us six tickets to the Ciné-Opéra. I never suspected a thing was wrong.

October 31st. Hallowe'en night. Jonathan and I, Élise, Quincey, and your mother's dear parents. We sat in the cinema as the lights faltered and died.

The title flitted on the screen.

Nosferatu le Vampire.

I held Jonathan's hand so tight. Hutter and Ellen. Ellen. It was me. My story. Torn from the pages of Stoker's book. Such a curious thing. No more than actors playing a role. I have seen a thousand plays. *Macbeth. King Arthur. Salome. A Doll's House.* Comedies. Tragedies. Actors and actresses taking the stage. But this? This did not feel like a play. It was a haunting. Spirits conjured on the screen. The ghost of Dracula at my throat, supping my blood.

No. This was a trap.

We took rooms on the third floor of the Hôtel Plaza Athénée, near the Théâtre des Champs-Élysées. We gathered weapons. Quincey's Lee—Enfield rifle, a revolver, a Luger and half a dozen butcher's knives.

I barely slept. The Luger Modell 1900 Parabellum sat by my bed. *Si vis pacem, para bellum - If you wish for peace, prepare for war.*

We woke in darkness. Élise was screaming.

Gunshots from the revolver, Quincey firing the rifle. Jonathan burst open the door, and we ran into your room.

I saw her then, stooped over your cradle. Ana—the vampire —a shape draped in black with your blood on her lips.

She slashed her hand open with a cut-throat razor, dripping her accursed blood onto your face.

Séraphine—my little one. Blood in your cradle, blood in your eyes and your mouth.

I fired the gun. Emptied the bullets into the vampire as she smiled at me.

Jonathan crashed headlong into the vampire, digging a carving knife into her body as they tumbled, together, shattering the window. They fell to the street, impaled on the spikes of the iron railings three floors below. Ana was gone before I reached Jonathan, vanished into the night.

She hid a letter in your crib.

My name is Ana Florescu.

You will remember my village, Dimitrescu, in Transylvania. You, Ms. Mina and the others lingered there that night. Down from Castle Dracula you came, victorious, Dracula's blood on your knife and on your skin.

The three, beheaded and destroyed. Izabela Lupu, Lacramioara Fieraru, and my mother, Sofia Lazarescu.

Know that I will be revenged upon you all.

Ana Florescu, deathless, ill omened, Dracula's daughter.

She fed on you, Séraphine, my beloved, and suckled you on vampire blood.

I telephoned Lucy from Salpêtrière Hospital. If we have any chance to save your life we must act without delay. I gave your mother Élise a choice: stay in Paris to care for her husband

Quincey or come with me to Scotland to try to save their daughter.

Jonathan and Quincey will be well cared for. Their broken bones will knit, their bloody wounds will heal. I pray that I will see them both again but if I die to save you, I will be content. You must not die Séraphine. You have to stay alive.

Extract from The Lancet Medical Journal, Volume 199, Issue 5151, May 1922

CONVALESCENT BLOOD TRANSFUSION IN INFLUENZA PNEUMONIA: OBSERVED DURING THE PANDEMIC OF 1918-1920

A lecture delivered at the Royal Institute of Public Health
Lucy Harker MBChB

The recent influenza pandemic is now known to have claimed more lives worldwide than all the battles of the Great War. This terrible mortality was opposed by a number of novel therapeutic measures. The transfusion of blood from convalescent patients to the acutely afflicted was observed to significantly reduce the mortality rate.

306 men, women and children died from influenza in Edinburgh in the week that the Armistice was signed. Around the world, soldiers carried the disease to their loved ones as they returned home. A dark purple and blue flush discoloured the skin: heliotrope cyanosis, caused by a lack of oxygen to the body as the lungs fill with pus and fluid.

The blood of recovered patients was drawn. It was thought that transfusions of this convalescent blood into the afflicted might provide some measure of immunity or fight the disease.

Lucy Harker's Diary

2 November 1922.—It was an hour before dawn. The telephone operator connected a call from the Salpêtrière Hospital in Paris. My mother asked if I had pen and paper. I was to note down what she told me. The words look like the ravings of a lunatic.

A vampire has bit Séraphine. It fed her its blood. If Séraphine dies, she will be un-dead, a vampire.

She will need blood. I am to administer transfusions. Nothing else will keep her alive. There is half a pint of blood in the body of a baby. I am to take a train south today to meet my mother, Élise and Séraphine at York, with a quart of blood.

They will leave Paris at first light. My mother has booked passage across the channel on the steamer Maid of Orleans. They will board a train at London King's Cross. heading north. After York, we travel on to Edinburgh's Waverley Station.

I am to meet this morning with John William Brodie-Innes. I am to remind him that he met my mother in London at the Isis-Urania Temple of the Hermetic Order of the Golden Dawn. I am to ask Brodie-Innes for the address of the Marquise d'Urfé.

Later—the train seems to inch along the tracks. I keep looking at my pocket watch.

I met Brodie-Innes in the library of the Scottish Lodge of the Theosophical Society, at 28 Great King Street. He told me that he was introduced to my mother by Constance Wilde. He is a lawyer, author and occultist. Founder of the Amen-Ra Temple in Edinburgh, the Alpha et Omega, and the Cromlech Temple. Brodie-Innes is a softly spoken gentleman, with silver hair and beard, and a neat Tweed suit.

He knows the truth about Dracula and has made a close study of the legends of the Scholomance and the art of necromancy. Reluctantly he gave me the address of the Marquise d'Urfé with a warning: she is treacherous and deceitful.

Mina Harker's Journal

3 November 1922.—I have not prayed to God since Beatrice died. But I prayed tonight.

God protect Séraphine. She barely lives.

She would not feed from her mother on the long journey north. Her chest heaved, each breath rattling. The colour faded from her face as we made our way to London and boarded the train. Séraphine did not cry. She scarcely made a sound, drifting into a fitful sleep. As I watched her, rocked in Élise's arms, I saw the dark blue of her veins scrawled across her skin.

I fell into Lucy's arms as she boarded our train at York. She took a bottle of blood from her doctor's bag and jabbed a needle into Séraphine's tiny arm.

As the blood ebbed into her body, Séraphine's breathing slowed. Her heart rate steadied, and her skin blushed: from ashen white to a rosy pink.

God help us. Séraphine consumed almost a quart of blood before we reached Edinburgh.

Lucy Harker's Diary

3 November 1922.—I have set up rooms at Surgeons' Hall, leaving Élise and Séraphine in the care of my friend Susan Anderson Binnie. She will administer blood transfusions while I take my mother to visit the Marquise d'Urfé.

Séraphine suffers from a high fever. Her pupils are unresponsive. I fear for her.

Mina Harker's Journal

3 November 1922.—The Marquise d'Urfé. 21 Regent Terrace.

We were met at the door by her servant, Pyotr. The house was dark, its windows kept shuttered, heavy curtains drawn. He led us up a grand staircase to the drawing room.

Many years ago, Brodie-Innes spoke to me of the Marquise in hushed tones. She dabbled in alchemy, he said, and necromancy. She kept one of the finest occult libraries in Europe. She studied the un-dead.

The drawing room was lit by candles and Tiffany lamps. The walls were covered in the most extraordinary collection of tapestries, paintings, antiquities and artefacts.

'Do you like my mask?' The voice was paper thin.

Lucy took a step back from the Japanese mask. It was red as blood, with horns and fangs.

'That is Shuten-dōji. A demon. He drinks the blood of maidens. Devours their flesh.'

The Marquise sat close by the fireplace. She wore silks, with a mink coat draped across her knees. Her face was in shadow.

'Madame Harker,' she rasped. 'Come close. My eyes are failing.'

I asked her to call me Mina, and introduced my daughter, Lucy.

'Mademoiselle.'

She shifted, uncomfortably, in her chair, wincing in pain as her spine bowed.

'Indulge me. Will you have some tea? I am fond of vervain and passionflower.'

She gestured to Pyotr, and he poured tea into a porcelain teacup.

'I need your help.' I tried to sound resolute.

'Yes,' she smiled. '*Tu es déjà mort*. I believe you do.'

'Mister Brodie-Innes tells me that you have studied alchemy, the elixir of life?'

Her laugh was hollow. 'The elixir. Do you believe in such foolish things?

'I do.'

She nodded. 'Sit. Take some tea. For the sake of your granddaughter, I will tell you the truth of it. And then, when we are done, we will part as friends, and you will owe me a favour.'

We sat and listened.

'My name is Jeanne Camus de Pontcarré de la Rochefoucauld de Lascaris, the Marquise d'Urfé.'

She sipped her tea.

'I was fascinated by the forbidden arts, becoming the patroness of alchemists and hermeticists. Have you heard of Jean Grosse? He was a German alchemist, a member of the French Académie royale des sciences. And there was the Conte di Cagliostro. And Casanova. They burned sulphur in their crucibles, ground cinnabar with pestle and mortar, distilled, and wasted half my fortune, but none ever made the elixir of life.'

She smiled. Her teacup clinked in its saucer.

'I met a Friar in London. Skin like dead leaves. He told me he was Donato d'Eremita di Rocca d'Evandro dell'Ordine di San Domenico. He had studied the alchemical arts in a laboratory at the Dominican Friary in Naples. He took the passionflower as his emblem. Its petals are Christ's apostles. Its filaments, the crown of thorns. Its three stigmas are the nails of the crucifixion and its anthers the five wounds.'

The Marquise wheezed, catching her breath.

'He had succeeded, making the elixir. He told me I would need valerian, cassia and cinnamon, mace, aloes, artemisia and honey, musk, bezoar stones, coral, pearls, sapphires, emeralds, gold and a hundred other things. He wrote it all in his book, *Elixir vitae,* in Naples, in 1624.'

Pyotr brought teacups and saucers. The Marquise paused as he poured us two cups of tea.

'I met d'Eremita in 1775. He was almost two centuries old. You see that painting, there by the window, that is d'Eremita. Painted by Caravaggio. I would have given all my fortune for the last dregs of the elixir, but d'Eremita gave it to me for nothing. It kept me alive all these long years, as my friends faded and died.'

She swirled the tea in her cup.

'I came to Scotland with the Duchess Marie-Thérèse Charlotte, the daughter of King Louis XVI and Marie Antoinette. The guillotine took their heads.'

The Marquise stared at me, meeting my eyes.

'I was born in 1705, and I have lived two hundred years.'

I leaned closer.

'Do you have the elixir?'

'No,' she shook her head. 'I took all there was. But I age. I do not know my face in the mirror. My hair is white. I am worn down to bone and skin.'

She laughed.

'Do not look disappointed. You may yet hope. The Friar d'Eremita told me of a Venetian apothecary that sold poisons and arsenic, opium, silver. The apothecary sailed with the Portuguese black ships to trade with Japan. He sought the elixir of life, following legends of Kaguya, a princess of the moon. She left the elixir of immortality in Japan, but the emperor had it burned on Mount Fuji—deathless mountain. Tales, rumours, lies.'

The Marquise tried to prop herself up, resting her elbow against the arm of the chair.

'The Venetian apothecary ate the flesh of a mermaid to stave off death. But you, you need the blood of a vampire. Its venom may cure the child, or it may kill her.'

She looked across at her servant. Pyotr nodded.

'There is a vampire, beneath the city. It is a troublesome thing. You must destroy it. Take its blood.'

'But…'

'Pour it into Séraphine's heart.'

Lucy flinched.

'Pyotr will lead you there.'

She slumped back in her chair.

'I will pray for you and your children, Madame Harker.'

Lucy Harker's Diary

3 November 1922.—We took weapons, arming ourselves with surgeon's knives and a Model 1903 Colt pistol. I carried my amputation knife. A steel blade with a nickel-plated handle, made by Down Bros. of London. My mother took the gun and a catling knife.

Pyotr met us at the foot of Candlemaker Row. Drunks were reeling out of the taverns, stumbling to the brothels, singing bawdy songs as they shambled by. There, backing onto the cobblestone street, was the high wall of Greyfriars Kirkyard. The graveyard was once the haunt of body snatchers, resurrection men that sold corpses for dissection at the university. I am thankful that the Anatomy Act meant there was a supply of legal cadavers during my studies.

Pyotr unlocked the door to a small shop that backed onto the graveyard. He led us through to a storeroom and took the padlock from an iron gate. He drew back a tattered curtain and stepped down some worn stone stairs into the dark.

The passageway wound down, beneath the tombs and burial plots. The walls of the tunnel were built of cobbles, robbed out bricks and ancient grave slabs. Skulls grinned out from the cracks in the walls. Tree roots wove their way through rib cages and curved around vertebrae.

The ground was damp, the stones wet underfoot. Pyotr said nothing as we descended. By the light of his lantern, I saw that he carried two Japanese swords. A katana and a wakizashi: the daishō.

After a hundred yards or so the tunnel opened out into a vaulted chamber. I had heard that there was a labyrinth of narrow alleys and ancient crypts beneath Edinburgh's Old Town. The floor was littered with broken bones, rags and shards of stained glass. A stone tomb lay close to one wall, its inscription worn away to nothing. I barely made out carvings of an hourglass and a winged skeleton.

'This way.'

I wondered if Pyotr broke the silence to steady his nerves.

'Where are the rats?' my mother whispered.

I hadn't noticed. It was odd. I was used to seeing rats in the gutters, running down by the canal. There were rats the size of dogs down at Leith Docks.

'It eats the rats.'

Pyotr stopped dead. The lantern light illuminating the cellars up ahead.

'Did you hear…'

The vampire fell on him, nails ripping open his trachea and carotid artery. Pyotr tried to scream, drowning in blood. Bodach they call it—the old man. Its skin was alabaster, eyes white, jagged teeth red with Pyotr's blood. It was naked, skeletal, skin stretched thin across bone. Its bare head was scarred and torn. I saw the mottled bone of its skull.

Mina Harker's Journal

3 November 1922.—I raised the gun and pulled the trigger.

There was nothing else I could do for Pyotr. His body slumped to the ground, knees buckling. The vampire stared out with blind eyes. The gun fired, a bullet piercing its skull an inch above its right eye.

The creature's head snapped back. It did not fall. Its head swivelled, to face me, grinning, smoke curling from the bullet hole in its forehead.

Lucy cried out and lunged forward, slashing at the vampire with her amputation knife. It raised an arm, the blade cutting its flesh, down to the bone. The vampire did not flinch. It leaned into the blow, snatching at Lucy. Raw-boned fingers closed around Lucy's throat.

Deathless. The vampire's fingers at my daughter's throat. Blood on her face, a vicious cut on her forehead.

I saw the katana at Pyotr's side. I threw myself forward, grabbing the hilt of the samurai sword and drawing it, out of its saya. I saw shining steel cut through the falling lamp and bite into the vampire's jaw. Its jawbone splintered, teeth shattering. The sword carved its eye in two and split its skull.

I felt no fear. Rage overwhelmed me. I was screaming as the sword arced down, slicing fingers from the vampire's hand, burying the sword deep in its body. Rib bones cracked. It snarled, vomiting pus as I hacked at its skull.

Lucy Harker's Diary

4 November 1922.—I wonder how we looked. My mother and I dragging the corpse of a headless vampire along Chambers Street to Surgeons' Hall. Blood running from the gash above my eye. We wrapped the pieces of its body in Pyotr's coat as best we could, buttoning it up and tying the sleeves.

Élise paced about the room, cradling Séraphine in her arms. Susan prepared to transfuse another quart of blood. The floor was littered with empty bottles.

Séraphine was fading. Her hunger was insatiable. Her fingers were a dark purple. Her body spasmed, her tiny heart racing.

I set the vampire's corpse on the operating table, making a vertical incision down the sternum. The stench of decay was overwhelming, its internal organs putrefying. Lungs blackened with necrotic tissue.

I broke open its thoracic cage, fracturing ribs as I dug out its heart.

There, pooled in its arteries, was the vampire's blood.

I must inject this abomination into Séraphine's tiny heart.

Mina Harker's Journal

5 November 1922.—I spoke with Jonathan on the telephone this morning.

Séraphine is healing.

Lucy's hands shook as she gave her niece the inky transfusion of vampire blood. She watched over her, night and day, as Séraphine fought with Death himself.

Last night Séraphine suckled at her mother's breast, tiny pink fingers holding tight to Élise's thumb. Her fever has broken.

I pray that Séraphine will be spared. After all she has suffered. If she dies, she will turn. God help us. This curse will hang over her head until Ana is destroyed.

I remember the words that Ana Florescu wrote.

'I will be revenged upon you all.'

Nothing will stop me. I will hunt this vampire to the ends of the earth. I will bury a stake in her accursed heart. Cut the head from her body. I will stuff her mouth with garlic flowers and stitch her lips shut.

I shall not fear.

Mark Oxbrow is a storyteller, author and ghostwriter. His short story, 'White as Snow, Red as Blood' was published by *Dracula Beyond Stoker*, accompanying Issue One. His story 'Frightful Things' published in *Dracula Beyond Stoker Issue 3: The Bloofer Lady*, was recommended by legendary editor Ellen Datlow as one of the best horror short stories of the year. Mark's books feature ghost stories, witch goddesses, Arthurian legends, poison gardens, folk horror, medieval monsters and secret treasures. Mark was born and raised in Edinburgh, the world's most haunted city. Over twenty-five years ago, he founded Scotland's largest Halloween festival.

Mother Mina
By Vince Stadon

When I first caught sight of Prana House, I assumed with lurching dismay that it had been almost entirely consumed by wild dense foliage and fallen into disuse. But when I looked more closely—craning out of the side window of the automobile as it neared our destination—I could see warm illumination from the upper windows and smoke plumes from a chimney, and to my relief the house appeared then to be a much livelier proposition. I quickly settled into my seat and readied myself for the interview, rehearsing what I might impress upon Mrs. Harker, my prospective employer, to sway the situation to my favour. I knew, for instance, that I would pretend to have taken several journeys by motorcar and that I had expected to have been greeted at the station by the driver, as if such dealings were commonplace. I would not mention my surprise and unease at learning that my driver was a young woman—French, from her accent; "Come, please, sit in the back, I will drive you," she had told me—and I would not remark upon the white robe she wore which was shockingly unsuited to her occupation. That dealings at Prana House (and perhaps all Greater London) were unconventional was becoming increasingly apparent to me, and I reasoned that my best tactic to ensure employment was to appear metropolitan; that is to say, outwardly detached and unaffected. This was a mask I was most comfortable wearing.

On foot, and with unwieldy luggage, I struggled to follow the French girl along a crooked, winding path. From all sides, wild bushes and trees loomed over; several times I was pricked by thorns or tripped on weeds. It was after 9'oclock and the early summer light was fading fast; the night was chilly, and I was glad of my overcoat. I thought my companion must surely be uncomfortably cold in her thin white robe, but she displayed no sign of it. It seemed to take an extraordinarily long time to reach the door. It was only when we were finally inside that I noticed she was barefoot. The French girl smiled at me, bid me adieu, and disappeared through one of the many doors that lined the room in which I now found myself. It was a large hall, perplexingly positioned at the rear of the house. There were potted plants everywhere, some so big they reached the high ceiling and had spread overhead. The effect was of a giant hand with leathery green fingers reaching down from above.

"Come with me," someone said, and I started with surprise. I snapped my head away from the ceiling and towards the voice. Another white-robed woman was standing by a door—a different door, I think, from which the French girl had exited. She turned and walked away, and I followed her along a gloomy winding hallway, lined with more giant plants, that weaved through the house and deposited us into an expansive sitting room that blinded me with its brightness as I stepped inside. I reflectively shielded my eyes. I heard a sharp sound, and suddenly, instantly, the blazing light was gone. I opened my eyes and saw that a curtain had been drawn. A window spanned the length of the room and now heavy green velvet curtains blocked the light, though here and there spears of light intruded into the room through gaps and tears.

"Forgive me," said a woman, stepping forward. "Moonlight can sometimes be as brilliant as a white-hot flame, particularly at this time of year. Please, do sit."

She gestured me to a chair and took another for herself. As she sat, the French girl and the other woman who had taken me here stood either side of her. Aside from the chairs and the women, the room was entirely bare.

"Mrs. Harker?" I had not spoken for so many hours that it felt odd to hear my voice.

"Please, call me Mother Mina," she said, and again gestured for me to sit. I did so and used the action as a sleight to study her. The most obvious thing was that she was with child and very near to full term. She rested her hands on her enormous belly. She too wore a white robe and was barefoot. She was strikingly beautiful, with raven-dark hair that fell in waves over her shoulders. She had dark eyes that glinted with secrets. Her voice was low and husky, but with charm and lightness.

"You have met Francine"—she gestured to the French girl— "and Amelia." The other girl raised an eyebrow. I nodded. I sat primly, my bag at my feet. I was tired and hungry from the journey, and it suddenly occurred to me that it was awfully late for an interview.

"Would you please show me your hands?" The question took me by surprise, and I had had no time to think about it before Mrs. Harker—Mother Mina—leaned forward to take my hands, and I let her, and when her warm hands took mine, I felt a shiver of intense pleasure that I could not explain.

"You have nice hands." Mother Mina smiled at me, and I could not help but return her warmth.

"Thank you, Mother Mina."

Mother Mina wiped away my tears (I had not known I was weeping) and then the interview was over, and Francine and Amelia led me out of the room and into the belly of Prana House and very soon I was asleep in a comfortable bed bathed in moonlight, where I dreamed of being born to Mother Mina.

ii.

I roomed with a timid Irish girl named Mary, who laid a white robe on my bed as she told me she had been born in a convent in Donegal and had made her way to England a year ago when Mother Mina had visited her in her dreams. I stared at the robe.

"I have my own clothes," I said, looking for my case.

"You'll not need them," said Mary.

"Where is my case?"

"You'll not need it."

"That is for me to decide." There was a snap to my voice, but the girl was becoming an irritant. Prana House was perplexing me.

"Mother Mina has decided for you," she said, as if a favour or a blessing had been bestowed upon me. Then Mary left the room, and I was glad to be alone.

Looked at in its true proportion, the events of last night could be rationally explained by tiredness and by dreaming. I had dreamed of a brilliant light and of weeping without knowing. I had dreamed too of the delight of being touched by Mother Mina. All else was the province of caprice and eccentricity and the strangeness of people.

That decided, I slipped into the robe and with a rumbling stomach, searched for breakfast.

The laughter of children guided me downstairs and out of the house into a hot garden so dense it might have been a jungle. There were giant ferns and waxy hoyas and banana plants and papaya trees, and brilliant orchids. Here and there were explosions of colour from every sort of flower. The greenery was wet from fresh rain and seemed covered in insects and birds, who provided a trilling undersong to the children's laughter. I caught glimpses of squirrels and rabbits and hares, ferrets, mice and cats and dogs and even deer. The impression was of a world within a world, bursting with life of every sort.

In the centre was a clearing that gave way to a giant circular stone table around which were about twenty women and as many children, though the children were restless and slipped away to run and play in the garden. Babies giggled as they rolled in the grass with dogs. Toddlers hopped clumsily with rabbits. Elder girls danced on tiptoes with deer. All the women wore white robes, amongst them Francine and Amelia and Mary. Several of the women were heavily pregnant. The table was laden with fruits and breads and berries. I had never seen so much fresh food.

"Help yourself," said Mother Mina, appearing behind me. She gently took my hand (again, I felt a thrill I cannot describe nor explain) and guided me to sit next to her.

"This is Nora," said Mother Mina, introducing me. "Welcome her."

"Welcome, Nora," said all the women and all the children together as they turned and smiled at me. Even the animals had become momentarily still. I felt unnerved.

"Nora has come from Derby to live here with us. She will take the room with Mary, where poor Daniella stayed, and she will take over from Daniella in the teaching of mathematics."

"Welcome Nora," said all the women and children once more. And then the stillness was broken, and Mother Mina broke a hunk of bread and offered me a piece.

The food was delicious, and I ate far too much as I listened to the gaiety of children and the industry of insects, and the songs of summer birds and I wondered what had happened to Daniella.

iii.

There were eighteen children, eight of them Mother Mina's. A few of the others were orphans. The youngest was a newborn girl named Ella. Prana House, I learned, was a school for children and adults and I was to teach both. It immediately struck me that there were no males of any age.

Of Mina Harker's brood, the eldest was a flighty eighteen-year-old named Lucy, who could speak an array of languages; the youngest, a two-year-old named Victoria. On my first morning Mother Mina decided the weather was too lovely to be indoors; we instead congregated in the garden, and I went from group-to-group learning names and how much mathematics they knew. In the late afternoon, Mother Mina insisted we all pose for a photographic portrait.

"We are joined by a new sister," she said, standing close to me, "and the occasion must be marked." Mother Mina gently rested my hand on her belly so that I might feel the baby kick as the flashbulb exploded.

A few days later I was gifted the photograph in an ornate silver frame. Seeing myself captured by photography was a new experience. I sat on my bed and examined the image with a magnifier. I noticed then a curious detail: every person in the photograph was looking not directly to the camera, but at me.

On Sunday morning I found Mother Mina at a typewriter. There was a stack of correspondence on the table. "A habit I have not grown out of," she said, by way of explanation. Next to the stack of letters was a photograph of a man in uniform. Mother Mina caught me looking. She picked up the photograph.

"My only son, Captain Quincey Harker. He is stationed in India."

I nodded and then cleared my throat. "Mrs. Harker… Mother Mina, I would like my case, if I may be permitted, so that I might wear my best dress to church."

"Oh, how quaint. But I am afraid we do not tend church here at Prana House."

"You do not go to church?" This was outrageous.

"Not in the traditional sense."

"You mean the Christian sense? The worship of God Almighty."

"There are many Gods."

I felt myself going red with anger. "I insist on this: there is only one true God." I could feel the heat of my words on my tongue. I was being insubordinate, but I did not care.

Mrs. Harker smiled and kept her voice as light as the air. "Life is all."

I did not know her meaning. I tried instead another tact. "Mother Mina, when I say my prayers in bed, I hear Mary say hers. Surely Mary attends Sunday worship?" It was inconceivable to me that an Irish girl would not be Catholic.

"You may *hear* Mary, but you have not listened," was all Mother Mina would say. Then she returned to her typewriter, and I knew I had been dismissed.

That night, I listened closely to Mary as she kneeled, head bowed, hands clasped before her. I could not at first make out her words, so quiet was her whisper. I moved closer, listened more carefully. And with a jolt, I heard her.

"Life is all. Life is all. Life is all. Life is all. Life is all."

iv.

Most evenings, when the children were in bed, we would sit in the garden around the stone table, and talk. Some of the women would drink wine. But I did not. I felt increasingly unmoored and bewildered. Prana House was a school but also much else. It was spiritual but not holy. It gave work to women but also set them free. I wore the white robe, but it did not suit me. I tutored children and adults, but I learned nothing in return. I sat with the women in the summer night, as fireflies charged the humid air with their luminescent loveliness, but I felt chilled and wintry in my very bones. And each time I resolved to leave, to flee back to Derby, or to anyplace that seemed of a place with the world as I had always known it to be, Mother Mina would hold my hands and I would feel such joy that I would be warmed in the blood, and my dreams would be of childbirth and of an enduring love that would outlast the world of men.

One night, without thinking, I took the glass when it was offered to me, and I was rewarded with a soft kiss by Mother Mina. I drank the wine, and I listened not to the women, but to the sounds of the night, and as I watched the red sun sink low into the azure sky, twinkling with stars, I found myself asking a question.

"What happened to Daniella?" I surprised myself with the directness of the inquiry.

The women stopped speaking. The sun was gone. Saturn was high in the night sky.

Mother Mina was sitting opposite from me, between Mary and a pretty Japanese girl named Naori. Mother Mina got up slowly from her seat, picked up a bottle, and padded over on her bare feet to sit next to me. She threw an arm around me, and as I thrilled to her touch, she said,

"Daniella sadly died in childbirth a few weeks ago." I could feel the pain in her voice. The other women bowed their heads.

I nodded. "And the child? Is that baby Ella?"

"Yes."

"Where is the father?"

Mother Mina refilled my glass. "He will be here soon."

There was palpable excitement from the women. The fireflies grew brighter.

And then talk turned to lighter matters, and we drank into the early hours. I had never before spent such a Sunday, and I wondered if something within me was changing.

v.

Over the next few weeks, I blossomed. The women became my friends and my instructors. From Irina, I learned to dance and to pick out a tune on a stringed instrument called a balalaika. From Francine, I learned how to bake bread and some rudimentary French. From Amelia, I learned to draw a bow and fire an arrow. I played with the children and learned from them how to be carefree and unafraid. I felt as if I had given myself completely to Prana House, and in doing so I was rewarded with feelings of such happiness and contentment. I laughed more than I had ever done so, even as child.

"This house is a house of life, and we live in its very breath," Mother Mina told me as I held her hand and stroked her face. "The word Prana means 'breath'. It means life itself. For life is every part of what we know to be real, and even what we dream." I gently wiped away her tears.

"You know so many things," I said.

"I have seen so many things. There is a darkness beyond all our understanding—a physical force of death—and even beyond death—that seeks to claim us and drain us of life and love. There are ways that are not our ways." She looked away, into the past, I presumed, and I could feel her fear and her resolve. And then a lightness came to her, and she smiled.

"But there is too, a blinding light," she said, in her low and husky voice, "a breath of life so powerful, so indestructible, so enduring it will drive away the darkness forever." Her eyes were shining. I knew then that I loved her.

"Life is all," I said.

"Life is all," said Mother Mina, as the baby kicked.

vi.

I was ready for the Master when he came to the house. There was a thunderstorm that night, but it had not awakened me; instead, I was stirred by Mary, holding a lantern.

"What is it?"

"It is time," she said, in an excited whisper.

Mary led me along the corridor, lined with all the other women. Mothers were holding their children. They smiled at me as I passed, patting me, touching me, some even kissed me.

I followed Mary into a large empty sitting room that at first blinded me, until I heard a sharp sound and when I opened my eyes, I saw Mother Mina seated, holding her newborn child, and standing behind her, her husband, the Master of the House: Mr. Johnathan Harker.

Mother Mina was soaking wet from sweat and the baby was crying as thunder crashed. When lightning flashed, spears of brilliant light cut through gaps and tears in the curtains.

I sat in front of Mother Mina and stroked her hair and cooed at the baby until both fell asleep. I could hear Johnathan gently breathing and the sound thrilled me.

I felt his hand gently pulling me to my feet, and then he lifted me into his arms. He was greying, but with a full beard and very kind eyes.

He carried me through a door into a small room filled almost entirely with a bed.

He kissed me softly as I undressed him.

I dreamed of a carriage speeding along a perilous mountain path in a land far away where the dead travel fast. Wolves howled and a tremendous thunderstorm ripped open a blood red sky.

When I awoke, I knew I was with child, and I had never felt happier.

The storm had passed, and the day was beautiful.

Alliance of Convenience
By Henry Herz

2 a.m., 17 July—Hampstead, Maryland

A dinged-up, gray Chevy G-series van rolled slowly through the affluent suburban neighborhood. Four men within the vehicle wore dark leather jackets, black pants, baseball caps, and work boots.

"What's the target doing now?" asked dark-haired, thirty-year-old Quincey.

Ted checked his GPS tracker. "He hasn't moved for the last minute."

Quincey tapped the driver's right shoulder. "Pull over here, Steve. We'll give him some time to get settled."

The red blip indicating the target car's location remained stationary for thirty minutes.

"Alright, let's go," ordered Quincey. "Dan, you bring the surveillance equipment."

The four men, each with a backpack, exited the van and walked two blocks. They spotted an indigo Aston Martin Vantage. The target's car was parked in front of an expansive, two-story Georgian Revival sided with red brick accented by symmetrical white-framed windows. The house was dark, the windows shuttered.

Cloaked by a cloudy, moonless night, the men slipped stealthily into the mature oak and maple trees of the back yard.

Thin strips of illumination leaked between the not-quite-closed shutters of a rear window.

"Dan," whispered Quincey, "stick a surveillance camera on that window."

Quiet as a mouse, Dan completed the task and returned. The four men put in Bluetooth ear buds. Quincey held a tablet computer now displaying the house's luxuriously appointed kitchen. The target and three strangers occupied the room, one of them lying unconscious, bound, and gagged.

"What the hell's going on in there?" whispered Quincey in the back yard.

The tablet showed a dark-haired man of indeterminate age standing behind their surveillance target, a tall, curly-haired man in a brown suit. The former held a thin sword under the throat of the latter, who maintained a surprisingly calm demeanor. When the dark-haired man's mouth began to move, Quincey increased the volume so he and his comrades wouldn't miss a word.

"Please have a seat, Mr. Christine. Ray, cover him."

"Yes, sir." A muscular man with reddish blond hair aimed his revolver at their target.

The target sat on a black leather bar stool and the sword-wielding man continued. "Please do not try anything, Mr. Christine. We have no wish to harm you, but know that Ray's revolver is loaded with hardwood cartridges. I should add that Ray is quite the accurate shot."

Having turned to sit and finally able to get a good look at his captor, the target stiffened in recognition. "Dracula! After all these years!" he cried in British Received Pronunciation.

Quincey's eyes bulged. "Holy shit!" he whispered. "In tracking Holmwood, we've stumbled on Dracula." His men nodded.

A smile brightened Dracula's countenance. "Indeed. Well, this night is full of surprises, Mr. Christine…or, I should say, the honorable Arthur Holmwood?"

Renfield's mouth fell open. "What?"

Dracula nodded. "I am as perplexed as you, Ray. Would you kindly elaborate for us, Mr. Holmwood?"

Arthur sighed. "After you turned Lucy into a vampire in London long ago, she fled. Soon thereafter, she yielded to the Urge and turned me. Although my soul was cursed, I deemed the price a fair one for being able to spend eternity with my beloved." His eyes glistened. "Tragically, our time together was cut short, because of Abraham Van Helsing, curse him."

Quincey scowled in the darkness.

Arther continued. "Failing to destroy you, Van Helsing hunted my Lucy. His dogged pursuit forced us to separate. I lost contact with my beloved and have sought her all these long years. My quest led me to this residence. Is she here? Tell me it is so, I pray you."

Dracula nodded. "She is indeed here, nearing the completion of a twelve-month sentence."

"Sentence?"

"Tell him, Ray."

"Decades ago, my master summoned the will to resist the Urge and to act for the benefit of humanity. He vowed to stop stalking strangers and draining their lifeblood. My master also insists that his vampire descendants do the same. I'm the latest generation in the line of faithful Renfields serving him. He sips my blood weekly, giving him the nourishment he needs, while leaving me human. When we found your wife Lucy a year ago, she did not share his… *philosophy.* She fed on children." Distaste marred Renfield's handsome face. "So, my master gave her a year to contemplate whether to follow his practice or to be staked."

Holmwood scowled and bunched his fists. "That is a bitter a choice. Still, I reached the same conclusion long ago to preserve what little remained of my soul."

Still brandishing his revolver, Renfield replied, "No offense, but you could just be saying that so we release you."

Dracula placed a reassuring hand on Renfield's shoulder. "His claim is verified easily enough." He removed the gag from the bound man lying on the floor, apparently Holmwood's thrall. Dracula gently shook him to consciousness and assisted him to a stool. He stared into the man's eyes, charming him into temporary compliance. "Tell me of your master's feeding arrangements."

The man's description of Holmwood's feeding habits confirmed his master's account.

"Well, well." Dracula smiled. "This is an unexpectedly positive development. Who better than her fiancé to help Lucy acclimate to a new...*lifestyle?* Arthur, if, without knowledge of your presence, she vows to only feed off the willing, then I will be pleased to reunite you with your betrothed."

Holmwood's face lit up like a child's on Christmas morning. "To see her would be the first true joy I have experienced in a century." Then worry wrinkled his brow. "I pray she makes the right choice."

"As do I." Dracula nodded. "Excuse me while I inquire of her decision." He left the kitchen.

Minutes later, Holmwood's eyes snapped to the right at the sound of footsteps.

Dracula, still out of sight, called, "I have wonderful news. Lucy has agreed not to prey on the unwilling. Lucy, we have a guest you will be pleased to meet."

Holmwood stood, trembling with emotion at the long overdue reunion.

Dracula led Lucy Westenra into the room, her arm hooked through his, not unlike a father giving away the bride at a wedding. Her steps were shaky from an eleven-month fast.

A slender blonde, Lucy was a stunning youthful-looking woman with pale blue eyes that went wide at the sight of her betrothed. Her mouth formed an 'oh' of wonder. "Arthur? Can it be?" she asked.

Holmwood rushed into the arms of his beloved, who tucked her head at his collarbone, not to drink, but to inhale the scent of her man. He stroked her long hair. The pair swayed like a couple slow dancing. He cradled her face in his hands, his thumb caressing her cheek, lost in her gaze. "Oh, Lucy! You are as beautiful as I remembered. How I have missed you!"

Tears rolled down their cheeks as they held the long-delayed embrace. Even Dracula's and Renfield's eyes glistened.

Holmwood eased his lips to Lucy's, offering a delicate kiss that was somehow both passionate and restrained.

In the backyard, Quincey scratched his head. "This is an incredible development. Strange as it seems, three vampires have removed themselves from our target list." His eyes lit with realization. "Maybe they can help us with a fourth vampire. We haven't seen Holmwood attack anyone in the last three weeks. Based on that and what we've heard, I think it's safe to introduce ourselves."

"Think? Safe?" asked Steve. "Are vampires ever safe?"

Quincey smiled. "I didn't say we shouldn't take *precautions*."

Nodding, the four men hung garlic and crosses around their necks. They armed themselves, pistols in holsters and wooden stakes tucked in their belts.

Quincey led them to the back door and knocked, the sound surreal under the circumstances.

Through the closed door, Renfield asked, "Who's here at such an ungodly hour?"

Quincey smiled mirthlessly. "Ungodly is right when dealing with vampires. We'd like a word with your master."

Dracula's eyebrows rose. "Interesting. Well, there is not much that can threaten three vampires and an armed assistant," he whispered. "Let us see what they want, Ray."

Revolver in hand, Renfield unlocked the door and backed up.

Four sturdy, grim-faced men advanced just inside the doorway. Their eyes flitted from vampire to vampire, and their right hands lingered near their wooden stakes.

Dracula appraised the newcomers in return. "Who are you?"

Being careful not to meet the Dracula's gaze, Quincey replied, "I'm the great-great-great-grandson of Abraham Van Helsing. I lead a team of vampire hunters."

Dracula's eyes widened. Lucy hissed and stepped back as Holmwood interposed himself between her and the men.

"You are brave, but perhaps foolhardy." Dracula unsheathed his sword.

Quincey raised empty hands in a calming gesture. "*However*, having overheard your conversation, we now have no quarrel with you."

The hint of a grin appeared on Dracula's face. "Indeed. Perhaps it is the converse that should concern you, Mr. Van Helsing. In any event, what is your business with us?"

"We propose working together to find Mina Harker. You know—beautiful brunette, bite marks on her neck, circular scar on her forehead."

Hatred twisted Lucy's fair visage. "Why? So you can destroy her? Long though the years have been, I still consider her my friend." She bunched her fists and leaned forward, her fangs lengthening.

Dracula extended a restraining arm. "Let us not be hasty. It is an unexpected but intriguing offer. Perhaps we can aid each other, since I wish to find Mina as well."

Quincey's head tilted. "You do?"

"Yes. We will ally *if* you agree that I may offer her the same choice as Arthur and Lucy. If she accepts, then you will stop pursuing her."

"And if she doesn't agree?"

Dracula shrugged. "Then I will not interfere in your *business* with her."

"No!" cried Lucy.

Holmwood took her in his arms. "My dear, think of Mina's soul. Should she not be offered the same opportunity to mend her ways as us?"

Tears formed in Lucy's eyes.

Quincey's and his men's shoulders relaxed. "Any thoughts on where we might find her?"

Dracula shook his head.

Arthur cleared his throat. "As I recall, Mina and Lucy holidayed in Whitby, England. Her maiden name was Murray, and her favorite wine was Châteauneuf-du-Pape."

"Not much to work with," commented Dan.

Quincey nodded. "Yeah, but it's all we have." He addressed the vampires. "Will you travel to Whitby?"

"My bride and I shall do no more." Holmwood took Lucy's hand. "We have a century of catching up to do."

"I am overdue to visit a friend in London anyway," Dracula replied. "Since my condition confines me to travel by ship, it will take Ray and I a week or so. As I recall, Middlesbrough has a port and is relatively close to Whitby."

"Good," replied Quincey. "While you're transiting, my men and I will fly over and sniff around. Will you notify us when you arrive?"

Dracula nodded to Renfield, who exchanged mobile phone numbers with Quincey.

17 July—Hampstead, Maryland

In the afternoon, Renfield made the logistical arrangements for he and his master. Via the internet, he leased an estate home in Middlesbrough's eastern suburbs, Renfield orchestrated transportation for a coffin and their equipment. Knowing his master's fondness for fast cars, he reserved an anthracite satin-colored Bentley Continental GT with a twin-turbo V8. Lastly, Renfield scheduled a meeting for the following week with Quincey at a long-established Middlesbrough pub.

4 p.m., 25 July—Middlesbrough, UK

When Dracula and Renfield entered the dimly lit Slaughtered Lamb, Quincey raised a beckoning hand from a corner booth. "I really appreciate you coming here and helping. First round's on me. What'll you have?"

Renfield tipped his head. "An amber ale."

"A Bloody Mary," said Dracula.

At Quincey's raised eyebrow, Renfield offered, "Yes, he does have a sense of humor."

"Okay, then." Quincey strode to the bar.

Renfield whispered, "I'm not sure about this guy. How do we know he's any good?"

Dracula touched his chest. "In his line of work, the fact that his heart still beats is testament to his skill."

After Quincey returned with their drinks, Dracula asked, "What have you been able to discover?"

Quincey sipped his frothy stout. "Of course, I didn't expect to find Mina Harker or Mina Murray listed in telephone directories, newspapers, or on social media, but we checked anyway. Nothing."

Dracula nodded approvingly. "One must be thorough."

"Then we canvassed local liquor stores to see if anyone regularly ordered Châteauneuf-du-Pape by the case. No luck there either."

"Go on." Dracula's face displayed no emotion.

"My team researched the locations of people who've gone missing over the last five decades. No patterns emerged." Quincey swallowed some stout as if to wash away the bitter taste of failure. "We checked property records for ownership of mansions within a twenty-mile radius. There were forty-seven, none owned by a Mina, Harker, or Murray."

Renfield frowned. "So, either no leads or too many."

Quincey nodded. "Right. We were stumped…until it hit me. If Mina held property in the area, she wouldn't want public records of a suspiciously long period of ownership by one person. That means she'd have to periodically create a new identity, buy the property under the new name, and then have the old identity 'die.'"

Dracula nodded, having used the same technique himself.

Quincey placed a file folder on the table. "Luckily, Dan's got a great eye for details and the tenacity of a bulldog. He compared the signatures of successive owners for each of those forty-seven homes." Quincey opened the folder. "These are photocopies of the title document signature pages for the last three owners of 17 Stainsacre Lane. As you can see, they are remarkably similar to each other. The current owner's name is Johanna Deane. The mansion's about five miles south of Whitby, nicely isolated on a ten-acre parcel."

Renfield leaned in. "Damn. Nice work."

"Indeed." Dracula smiled. "Let us now plan our visit—in daytime, so she cannot escape by transforming into mist."

1 p.m., 26 July—Whitby, UK

The Bentley Continental GT rolled up the private road, through an open wrought-iron gate, and onto a wide, circular cobblestone driveway. It halted under the mansion's porte cochere behind a parked Rolls-Royce Phantom and a Lamborghini Temerario.

Dracula exited the Bentley, wearing a bespoke black suit, white cuff-linked shirt, and a blood-red Hermès silk tie. Using an ivory-handled walking stick, he feigned a limp, ascended five broad marble steps, and knocked on the massive, carved oak doors.

A young man opened a door. "Good afternoon, sir. May I help you?"

Dracula offered a gleaming smile. "Sir Henry Irving for Ms. Deane. I regret that the urgency of my visit did not afford me time to schedule an appointment."

The servant's eyes widened at the title. "Very well, sir." He gestured to the travertine-floored foyer and stepped aside. "If you would be so kind as to take a seat, I will see if she is available."

After the man departed, Dracula surreptitiously unlocked the front door and retook his seat.

The servant soon returned. "If you would please come with me, sir." He led Dracula through the luxurious manor to a huge, rectangular room. The high-ceilinged mahogany-paneled space measured one-hundred feet long from north to south. A doorway stood in the center of each wall. They passed through the doorway in the fifty-foot-wide southern wall. Numerous large pieces of furniture adorned the room—ornately carved armoires and credenzas, stout bookcases filled with leather-bound tomes, a ten-foot-long wooden dining table with eight high-backed chairs, luxuriously upholstered sofas with matching ottomans, and a black grand piano.

Perhaps thirty feet from the southern doorway stood a maroon velvet settee, an ornate Brazilian rosewood coffee table, and a brown leather Chesterfield chair facing the settee, its back to the doorway. On the settee lounged an elegant, young-looking woman wearing a flowing green silk dress. She had long, wavy brown hair and green eyes. "Please have a seat, Sir Irving." She gestured gracefully to the chair. "May I offer you some wine?"

Dracula sat and dipped his head. "You are too kind, Ms. Deane."

The servant pulled a mobile phone from his pocket, pushed a button, and handed it to his mistress.

"Hello, Charles. We have a guest in the ballroom." She offered Dracula a smile. "I would like hors d'oeuvres and a bottle of Vouvray." After a pause, "That is correct, Vouvray." She handed the phone to the servant, who departed. Engaging Dracula in polite chitchat about the weather and the state of economic affairs, she revealed a keen mind.

Soon, six servants entered the room from the eastern doorway bearing covered silver food platters. They halted fifteen feet from Dracula, forming a circle around him and Ms. Deane. From under their shirts, they withdrew necklaces strung with a crucifix and garlic. The men tossed aside the cloches, seizing a wooden stake in each hand. None made eye contact with Dracula.

Dracula remained seated. "Ah, Mina. So you remember me after all this time. I am flattered."

A scowl marred Mina's elegant face. "I will never forget you or forgive you! By making me a vampire, you denied me the chance to have children with my beloved Jonathan." She shifted in her seat, mastering her anger. "Out of curiosity, why did you come here?"

"First, to express my deep regret for turning you. I know it does not repair the harm caused, but perhaps it will offer a sliver of consolation."

Mina snorted. "Cold comfort indeed."

"I also wished to let you know I have mastered my predatory inclinations. Now, I only feed from a single, willing assistant—never enough to kill him or create a new vampire. Will you consider adopting the same philosophy? Lucy Westenra and Arthur Holmwood have done so." Slowly, he withdrew a recent photograph from his jacket pocket and slid it across the coffee table between them.

Mina picked up the photo. "Lucy…" She traced her finger over the image, and her expression softened. "My old friend…" She sighed wistfully. "I should dearly love to see her again. Where does she reside?"

"I will happily tell you…if you agree to henceforth resist the Urge."

Mina looked up from the photo and tilted her head. "And if I do not?"

Dracula lowered his voice. "I am afraid that to prevent you from creating more vampires, I would regretfully need to destroy you."

Seething hatred returned to Mina's expression, and her eyes flicked to her obedient thralls. "My men may have something to say about that." Mina's grin contrasted disconcertingly with the fury burning in her eyes. "You have not offered me much incentive, but there may yet be a way you can help me to cease feeding on humans. My understanding is that if you are destroyed, I will revert to being human. Of course, with such arcane matters, one never knows until one tries."

"Indeed." Dracula offered a grin of his own. "Though my men may have something to say about that."

The tactical throat microphone concealed under Dracula's suit lapel had conveyed the entire conversation to his comrades. Renfield and the vampire hunters, Quincey, Dan, Ted, and Steve, had waited a quarter-mile away in a rented Mercedes-Benz EQS electric SUV. Upon Dracula's mention of six armed men, they drove the SUV silently to the mansion's unlocked front doors. From there, they slipped in and split into two groups. Renfield and Quincey stealthily took up a position outside the southern door. Ted, Dan, and Steve crouched outside the western door.

"Ray, if you would be so kind," Dracula called out.

Renfield and the others leaned into the two doorways, exposing only their heads and guns. The vampire hunters wore Interceptor multi-threat body armor and crucifix/garlic necklaces similar to the ones used by Mina's thralls. They held SIG SAUER P320-Flux Legions—pistols with two thirty-round magazines and a telescoping shoulder brace. Large hunting knives hung from their belts. Slung across their backs were Cobra Rx Adder tactical repeating crossbows. Instead of carbon fiber bolts, the six-round magazine held cocobolo hardwood bolts.

Renfield held a Glock 17 pistol with a thirteen-round magazine of 9mm silver-tipped rounds...because you just never knew. A Smith & Wesson Model 500 .50-caliber five-shot revolver with a 7.5" barrel hung at his right hip. Instead of body armor, a camouflaged nylon tactical vest with Modular Lightweight Load-carrying Equipment webbing covered his torso. Its pouches held spare magazines for the Glock, speed loaders for the revolver, garlic pepper spray, and a sheathed M3 trench knife. The vest's webbing prominently displayed a silver crucifix on Renfield's chest, another on his back.

Vampire Hunting 101—Guns to clear the thralls, then stakes for the vampire. This was not the former U.S. Ranger's first rodeo.

The two vampires remained seated, staring at each other. "Leave now if you want to live," Dracula warned Mina's servants.

Normal humans would have heeded Dracula's admonition.

These six were not normal humans, being fully under Mina's influence and unshakably loyal.

At a subtle dip of Mina's delicate chin, the four thralls positioned behind her retreated toward the center of the room for the cover offered by sturdy wooden furniture. Drawing pistols from the back of their belts, the four opened fire at Quincey, Dan, and Steve, wasting no rounds on Dracula. The gunshot reports echoed off the wood-paneled walls.

A bullet slammed into Steve's chest. His armor prevented it from penetrating, but the force still knocked him backward. Ted and Dan returned fire.

During the exchange of gunfire, the two thralls positioned behind Dracula's chair charged him, lunging with their wooden stakes.

Renfield fired two rounds into one man's back. The thrall grunted and fell, his stakes tumbling under the coffee table and his blood staining a Persian rug. Renfield pivoted to fire at the other thrall. Before he could aim, the man stabbed the left side of the still-seated Dracula's back, aiming for his heart.

The ceramic-coated compressed-polyethylene cuirass concealed under Dracula's shirt turned the blow. A vicious upward backhand from the vampire struck the thrall's jaw, producing an audible crack. The man tumbled backward onto the carpet.

Dracula and Mina stood, eyeing each other warily, heedless of bullets that could not harm them.

Ted, Dan, and Steve exchanged fire with the other four thralls. Neither the furniture behind which the minions crouched nor the wall behind which the vampire hunters ducked could stop bullets. But odds favored the vampire hunters, who had body armor and more ammunition.

Ted took a round to his mid-section, the blow knocking the wind out of him.

Dan picked off a thrall with a well-aimed headshot.

Steve unloaded five rapid-fire shots through a cabinet to take out another.

Crouching near Renfield outside the southern doorway, Quincey swapped his pistol for his crossbow. "That's four thralls down."

Raising an eyebrow, but keeping his attention on the gunfight, Renfield replied, "I prefer the term *assistants*."

In all the cacophony, Ted, Dan, and Steve did not hear a slightly built man creep up behind them. A powerful swing of his kukri lopped off Steve's head. It tumbled into the room. Dan had time only to scream before the assailant pivoted and stabbed him in the heart, affording Ted a chance to escape down the hallway toward Quincey and Renfield.

At the death of his men, Quincey's face reddened with fury. "He's mine, Ray."

The grinning murderer stepped over Steve's body, pausing in the western doorway to savor the chaotic scene. Blood dripped from his blade, and his eyes blazed.

Ignoring Quincey's request, Renfield fired twice at the man with the kukri, after which his pistol slide locked open, empty. The shots struck the man's chest but only seemed to antagonize him. Holstering his pistol and drawing his revolver, Renfield warned his comrades, "He's a vampire!"

Mina offered Dracula a smile that Judas in Hell might be proud of. "Surprise! You remember my husband, Jonathan Harker, do you not?" She closed her eyes and mumbled briefly.

Breathing hard with terror in his eyes, Ted raced around a corner and joined Quincey and Renfield.

Quincey whispered, "Ray, keep Jonathan's attention on you. Ted, switch to your crossbow and follow me. We'll go back the way you came and flank that bloodsucker."

Ray nodded his agreement, and the two vampire hunters slipped around the corner.

Moments later, growls from behind sent a surge of adrenaline coursing through Renfield's veins. He spun. Two enormous, slavering wolves, summoned by Mina, charged. Their claws gouged the hardwood floor.

"Shit!" Renfield only had time to pivot to protect his right side.

The wolves slammed into him, jarring the revolver from his right hand and knocking him to the floor. Jaws clamped like vices on his left shin and left forearm. The yellow-eyed wolves jerked their heads savagely from side to side, which would have torn apart the flesh of unarmored prey. However, under his clothing, Renfield wore a Kevlar chainmail shark suit…because you just never knew. The wolves exerted crushing pressure on his limbs. Shaken violently, his eyes locked on his foes, Renfield reached blindly for a weapon with his right hand. Unable to reach his fallen revolver, he yanked the trench knife from his vest and stabbed a wolf's neck several times until it went limp. He did the same to the other snarling wolf.

Without looking at her husband, Mina shouted, "Finish off the humans, dear. Then we can give Dracula the welcome he deserves." She knelt to seize one of the stakes dropped by a thrall. Madness tinged her laughter. She took a leisurely step toward Dracula.

Renfield released his gory knife, snatched up his revolver, and stood. Adopting a Weaver Stance for accuracy, he fired, the thunderous boom distinct from the crack of pistol fire.

A half-inch-diameter magnum round of sharpened Brazilian olive wood struck Mina's sternum at two-thousand feet per second. She howled, and the wound sizzled, but she remained standing. Her eyes turned black with rage.

Renfield adjusted his aim slightly and fired again.

Mina's eyes went wide when the hardwood bullet pierced her heart. She stood rigid, as if in shock.

Dracula drew the hidden rapier from his cane and slashed in one smooth motion, the blade barely visible.

Mina's body and head tumbled to the floor separately. No blood flowed. Dark smoke marked her passage into Hell, leaving behind only two piles of ash.

"No!" screamed Jonathan, at the final death of his wife.

The two surviving thralls retreated to the northern doorway.

As Jonathan stormed toward Dracula with the fury of a hurricane, wooden crossbow bolts fired from the western doorway struck his left shoulder blade and lower back. The wounds crackled.

Quincey and Ted grunted as they levered the crossbow's loading bar, which extended from a hinge at the bottom of the fore-grip to the bottom of the pistol-grip, chambering another bolt from the magazine.

Renfield fired his revolver, the wooden round striking beneath the distracted Jonathan's left clavicle—dangerously close to his unbeating heart.

Dracula raised his rapier to the ready position. He beckoned Jonathan with his left hand.

Jonathan scowled. "I shall take my revenge at another time, Dracula." He spun and raced toward the northern door. Wooden crossbow bolts and bullets struck the paneling on either side of the doorway. "Delay them," Jonathan commanded the two remaining thralls. He sprinted down the corridor, two bolts still protruding from his back.

"Kill the men so we can destroy Jonathan," Dracula ordered

Renfield, Quincey, and Ted laid down a barrage of pistol fire from two different directions. Fifteen seconds later, the two thralls lay dead.

During that time, Jonathan slipped through a sliding wall panel and into a hidden corridor.

Quincey and Ted rearmed with crossbows, and Renfield swapped his pistol for his stake-firing revolver. They followed Dracula down the northern hallway until he halted at a T-intersection. Jonathan was nowhere to be seen.

Pursed lips formed on Dracula's normally placid face. "We will search the house. Stay close."

Five minutes later, when the hunters reached the kitchen, distant gunshots rang out.

Dracula's eyes widened. "Our prey has fled outdoors. With me!"

Weapons ready, Dracula and his comrades eased out the mansion's front entry, eyes sweeping from side to side.

"Well, that is unfortunate." Dracula sighed and sheathed his blade.

The men followed his gaze toward the driveway. The Rolls-Royce, and the rented Bentley and Mercedes-Benz sagged slightly, their rear tires shot out. The Lamborghini was gone, no doubt driven by Jonathan. "We have no way to give chase."

Quincey swore. "We lost Steve and Dan, and failed in our mission." Regret twisted his face.

"Your team acquitted themselves admirably and helped destroy one vampire," Dracula replied. "It is a shame Mina did not accept my offer. That would have saved the lives of your men and hers."

Quincey spat. "Ted and I'll search for coffins we can *spoil* with holy communion wafers. And we've gotta figure out what to do about poor Steve's and Dan's bodies."

Dracula dipped his chin. "I have a discreet *contact* in Manchester who can be of assistance in that regard."

Quincey shuddered at the implications. Even if the wolf agrees to dwell with the lamb, the lamb is understandably nervous.

Author's Note

Isaiah 11:6—"The wolf will dwell with the lamb, and the leopard will lie down with the goat."

Readers may be tickled to learn that there is a "Dracula Experience" attraction in present-day Whitby.

This is the sixth adventure of occult detectives Dracula and Ray Renfield, whose covert exploits are documented in "Norsemen Cruise Line," *Dracula Beyond Stoker (DBS) issue #1*, "Don't Mess With a Renfield," *DBS #2*, "Loose End," *DBS #3*, "Cold Shoulders," *DBS #4*, and "Smitten," *DBS #5*.

Henry Herz has written for *Daily Science Fiction, Weird Tales, Pseudopod, Metastellar, Titan Books, Highlights for Children, Ladybug Magazine,* and anthologies from Penguin-Random House, Albert Whitman, Blackstone Publishing, Third Flatiron, Brigids Gate Press, Air and Nothingness Press, Baen Books, *Dracula Beyond Stoker*, and elsewhere. He's edited nine anthologies and written fourteen picture books. www.henryherz.com

Reclamation
By Bill Cozza

The mist wafted beneath the door, pale and dense, permeating the room with its foulness. It flowed freely, billowing with intention, as if sentient, and certainly hungry. Within the mist pulsed a light, subtle but brilliant, strobing like a heartbeat as the fog spread like a curtain across the room. Outside, the sounds of the asylum were muted by the swelling thump of that heartbeat. It curled across the floor, swiping at the bed skirt and climbing, clawing for the couple asleep above. He, sleeping like the dead from exhaustion after days of action. She, sleeping uneasily despite the draught she had taken, now waking, sensing a shift in the room. Clearing the blur from her vision as she craned her neck, she acclimated to the darkness around her. And her breath caught.

Swirls of thick white mist surrounded the bed, rising so high that it blotted out the window beside them. From where she lay, she could not see beyond the foot of the bed, and she thought for a moment that she must still be dreaming. But then, just beyond an arm's reach, unpeeled two ruby, ravenous eyes. In them lived no kindness, no recognition, no reason. Only hunger, and death. They stared, boring into her, for ages, and she could do nothing but stare back until she could bear the weight of their gaze no longer and finally thought to call out, to scream, to run. But she could not do any of that.

The pulsing light in the mist kept time with her own heartbeat now, flashing faster and faster. All the while those horrid eyes lingered. Then came the voice, breathy and feminine, not the voice of the creature behind the eyes.

Unclean.

She moved to wake her husband but stopped short, knowing inexplicably that if she were to rouse him, it would be a death sentence. The creature loomed eagerly, waiting for her to do it. She would not give him to it. The eyes seemed closer, hungrier, when she looked back. Beneath them, a skittering filled the room, like hundreds of claws running across the floor. Rats, she thought, hundreds of rats, wading over every inch of the wood below. Running more eagerly and furiously with every second, accentuating the movement of the eyes, which now drew nearer. Mortifyingly slow, they advanced, growing wider and redder.

Unclean…

She was lost in those damned eyes, in the hypnotic light, in the deafening skittering. It felt like losing herself, as if she'd fallen right into the crimson pools. She wanted the mist to envelop her and keep her concealed, even as the figure in the fog grew clearer, manifesting fully beside her, those hungry eyes so close that she could feel its breath. Her husband still did not stir; there would be no chance for goodbyes. She barely registered the pain. The pulsing light shone vibrantly as she then tasted copper.

Unclean!

I awake from my dream with a gasp, my forehead dotted with sweat in spite of the cool autumn breeze from my window. I have kicked the blanket from the bed, but I have no need for it as I take stock of my surroundings. No mist, no bloody eyes, just my empty bedroom. This is not a new dream, I have had it—or similar to it—for the past twenty-seven years. Those years ago, it was much more of a problem, and a more recurring presence in my life, but of late I dream it perhaps every couple months. What once caused awful night terrors and fits of paranoia is now nothing more than a gasp upon waking, for which I am grateful.

People are fond of saying that time heals all wounds. I don't believe that's true; some wounds are never fully healed—but they do become easier to live with.

Our ordeal was so long ago, sometimes it is hard to believe nearly three decades have passed. There are finally days that I do not think of my experiences at all, though they are seldom. It's difficult to fully forget, made even harder by the public's knowledge and obsession with the tale. Some days I curse the moment Arthur suggested we entrust our pages to his friend. An author, he told us, who could help get the story out. Warn the public of the darknesses in the world. Instead, we became an oddity and a sensation. The public wasn't warned; they were *entertained*.

Soon enough it was as though every pair of eyes in the Kingdom was upon us. We couldn't go to the theatre without being leered at. Parents began to have reservations about their children being taught by such a *controversial* figure and would pull them from my care. Jonathan's firm became a momentary target for the newspapers and a punchline around town. Thankfully that didn't last long, and his position became more secure.

As I stretch and greet the dawn shining in through my window, I think of our friends. Van Helsing, the dear, poor man, was laughed out of the country, but was welcomed back in Holland with great celebration. He continued to teach and practice there, and we often wrote each other until he passed away almost ten years ago now. Jack and Arthur both got through the spectacle unscathed, successful, married family men. While we were happy for them, there was some bitterness, admittedly, that we became so ridiculed and they did not. Neither man would know what we did about how complicated it was to raise a child under such scrutiny: their children would have an easier time finding friends than our Quincey had. Just as my pupils' parents had, the parents of Quincey's schoolmates had reservations about associating with us. Arthur and Jack, with their high standing, could not relate.

I last saw them about seven years back, at Jonathan's funeral.

We lived happily, with love, but the poor man was robbed of precious time by those creatures. Quincey kept him young as long as his body would allow, and oh how he loved fatherhood. To see him play and laugh with our son brightened any day. But each passing year seemed to take double the toll on him. He passed peacefully, surrounded by love and light.

Today I have been invited to tea with a dear friend, one Jonathan never had a chance to know, but whom I have no doubt he would adore. I believe he'd feel as I do, that my friend would remind him of Mr. Morris.

Jonathan's passing opened the door, after all we had experienced, for a fresh start. Quincey would be starting in a new school soon, and the prospect of going somewhere we weren't as known was never more appealing. There had been some early attempts to turn Mr. Stoker's novel into a play, which brought the attention all back again. From the West End all around the city, the tale was being told anew, this time heavily edited. It appeared some of the drafts were adding a romantic element, casting the "Mina" character—that's all I'd become to most of the country, a character—as the damsel in distress, attracted to the monster's magnetism, caught between men.

The glances I found freshly upon me now held an added judgment. The insult of this characterization seemed to bother the playwriters not at all. And once British society has its mind made up about you, it is futile to argue your case, especially if you do so in a dress. I thought it best to leave before a company got a production underway.

So, within a few months, with our savings, and all Jonathan had left us, we boarded a ship and began a new life in New York. Arthur generously gifted us a modest amount to help until we got settled and I could find a new position teaching, which did not take as long as I was expecting. New York was kinder to some immigrants than others, and for some reason the English were amongst the groups having an easier time. I had wonderful new pupils, Quincey settled into his new school, found friends much more easily, and excelled in his classes, of which I know Jonathan would be proud.

People in America still knew the story, but either they didn't immediately know us to be a part of it, or they came to the conclusion slower. We found our happiness again.

Of course, my dreams still came, but the new location provided a brief respite. There were no longer reminders around every corner, hiding in the shadows.

Before long, Quincey came to me with a decision about his career—to think our boy was nearing university age already made me feel the years. He would, he told me, follow in Jonathan's steps and study the law. When the time came, he was accepted as a student at Harvard University. A mother has never been prouder, and the look of pure joy on his face at the news made my heart swell. We might be out of our class at Harvard, but I would spare no expense for him and his desires. Jonathan and I had done well and saved plenty, I lived modestly, Quincey would be okay. Though I would miss him.

The thought of him going away stirred up a pang in my memory, as the last time someone I loved went away from me for so long was when Jonathan left for those cursed mountains. The nightmares returned then. But I pushed them away. This was Massachusetts, not Transylvania, a mere train ride away, and he was going to university, not to the belly of a monster (but then, I hadn't known Jonathan was going to the belly of a monster at the time, had I?).

It was at Quincey's orientation at Harvard that I met a kindred spirit. At the time, I was feeling out of place, seemingly the only single mother on campus to help her son acclimate, surrounded by important-looking men and pairs of parents. I couldn't help but keep to myself, feeling like a bear in a tearoom. Some parents made idle talk with me throughout the day, but I could feel the inquisition behind their eyes. *Where is your husband?* I'd become used to such inquiries, especially with some of my recent associations. But those judgements only fueled me. I had in the past couple years met a group of politically active working women—suffragettes—lobbying for equal rights and voting rights for women, and I was fully embraced into their cause and their community. It gave me a purpose I had lacked in England, and furthermore it brought me new companionship. But such is the way with our cause, every day on the street we see the same look on the faces of passersby. The judgement that we should be out, women, being *noticed. Heard* as well as seen. They always want to ask, *Where is your husband?*

But by the end of the day at Harvard, I remember Quincey's excitement as he came to introduce me to his new friend, someone he'd got on with immediately, fast and fiercely. He brought to me a strapping lad, lean and tall, with broad shoulders and a noticeably long forehead but a dashing smile that drew all attention. I felt I had seen this boy before.

"Mom," said Quincey. "This is Quentin."

"A pleasure, ma'am," Quentin expressed as he took my hand. "Your son is possibly the least boring person in this new class." Then he motioned behind him, waving for someone to join us. Like an aristocrat, Quentin began an introduction. "If I may, I'd like to introduce you to my parents."

I knew his parents on sight. His mother, a handsome woman, with a kind face, but one that belied that she could be venomous if crossed. She embodied poise, her wide hat blotting out the sun with its impeccable feather arrangement. His father was a bull of a man, tall and broad—the body of an old soldier for sure—moving with determination but also with a joyful bounce in his stride. His rimless glasses and finely groomed moustache were recognizable, but none so much as the beaming, toothy smile on his face.

A bear paw grasped my hand as he boomed, "Mrs. Harker!" The former President emphatically pumped my arm as he introduced himself. "Theodore Roosevelt, my wife Edith, we are truly *de*lighted to meet you!"

L ike our sons had, Theodore and I became friends instantly. He is a kind and empathetic man with a huge heart, his spirit outweighing even his grand personality. Edith and I became friendly, but it was Theodore who took a particular interest in my company. I knew right away it was from his adventurous spirit; he was not shy about knowing my story—or at least the public accounts of it. It turned out, Theodore had been a distant acquaintance of Mr. Stoker's. They'd met when Stoker was in America on business and had corresponded a few times while he was publishing his novel.

Theodore told me once he'd pressured Stoker to introduce him to the real authors of the pages. "I told him, *Abe*—he hated me for it, he went by Bram, but I couldn't help but put an elbow in his rib—*Abe, you've got something great here, but you might have changed their names for their sake. You must put me in contact with them.* But he wouldn't, he always said, *Lord Godalming values his privacy, and he surely wouldn't provide me with his friends' addresses.* It's a bully story, truly, and I have longed to hear more about it."

I quickly found Theodore to be a collector of strange stories, having more than one of his own. The great frontiersman he was, an accomplished explorer, he'd met some oddities along the way, and he lit up when talking about them. He tired so quickly of the small talk of his class—he had no interest in finance beyond a great many complaints, and his colleagues seemed to only want to talk about their money, the country's money. He animated while discussing politics, his passion for progress obvious. Beyond my encounter with that creature, he claimed to have become aware I was in New York through my work with the suffragettes. "A bully cause," he called it. "It's high time we modernized this country and gave women a proper voice." His work toward women's inclusion was an aspect of his politics I'd admired even from across the Atlantic. With his influence, I felt we could do some excellent work together.

But it was exploration where his conversation became truly alive. And he'd long desired, he told me, a conversationalist who wouldn't judge his outlandish stories. We understood each other in that. Theodore knew me; he'd spoken about me and wanted to meet years ago. There was no judgement at all from him of my account. I could confide in him.

It took some time, but he deepened our trust with his own accounts—or those he'd collected—of the weird things in the world. He shared a story from a guide he'd once traveled with, who had encountered a large hairy thing in the wilderness, something that was becoming known as *Bigfoot* ("Stupid name, terribly uninspired"), though they could never be sure it was the same beast. He shared with me the accounts of the Snallygaster, a dragon-like beast, massive in wingspan, and reptilian but for its immense claws like steel hooks. This beast supposedly terrorized parts of Maryland during his presidency and became so publicized that the Smithsonian issued a reward for its hide. Papers had written it off as a hoax, but Theodore had seen evidence to the contrary. "It was hushed up to stop the public from panicking, but the beast was very real, and very deadly." While it had been publicized that he considered postponing a trip abroad to hunt it, what wasn't public was that he'd had the beast found and killed quietly. He must have seen the disbelief on my face because he smirked at me, went to his desk and came back with a severed scale of reptilian flesh and a tremendous talon. His last story, though, convinced me of his genuine ability to believe mine.

During his account of a hunting trip in Washington State, his expression grew grave, his playful demeanor changed entirely. This was many years ago, he and a friend had employed a Native guide for their expedition through the wilderness. At a point, they came across a densely wooded area. "The air here changed, it was thicker, like filled with an invisible smoke. Our guide stopped walking and pleaded with us not to go into this patch of the forest. He told us that this part of the forest was the domain of an evil spirit, something his people knew to be savage and unforgiving. It would be offended, he said, if we entered its territory. At the time, I was not so open-minded, and I figured he was hiding something from us, valuable game or something his people didn't want us to find, so I insisted we push on. I was wrong. There was no game to be found in this area. We trekked for hours and saw only birds in the trees. By the time we decided to move on, night was falling, so we camped for the night. Our guide grew more anxious by the minute, and insisted we camp elsewhere. But no, I told him, this business about an evil spirit was malarky and we would camp here. But I tell you, the fire that night cast the strangest, most ungodly shadows, and from inside my tent we heard noises no man or beast I'd even encountered could make. I find them impossible to describe to this day, but to say they were the sounds of Hell."

I saw such vulnerability in Theodore that day as he shared such stories with me, maybe as eager to have someone believe him as I was for someone to believe me. So, over drinks, late into the evening, I recounted my story. The truth is that Stoker published our pages exactly, nothing omitted, so there is not much more to tell than what it seems everyone has read about what transpired that year. But Theodore wanted to hear from a first-hand source. So, I told him everything, from Jonathan's imprisonment in the castle to the shipwreck, poor Lucy's affliction and death to my attack in the sanitorium. He particularly sat forward as I detailed our dual journeys from London to Transylvania, trying desperately to cross the terrain before the Count. It made sense that he'd be interested in the travel and the horseback action. But he showed true empathy when I explained what it was like to have my mind connected to the Count. The violation, the feeling of being out of my body, the revulsion at feeling so close to it. Having full control of one's body is something we all take for granted, until a day when that power is taken from you, and only when you've regained control can you truly appreciate what a gift it is. Perhaps, I told him, that is why I've drifted toward the fight for women's rights. Having a new appreciation for my control over myself, the idea of being bound by other people's laws— men's laws—with no say in them myself is as revolting as being psychically connected to a monster.

At that, Theodore nodded his head, completely hearing me, and understanding as much as anyone (indeed, any man) could.

I told him about our summertime trip to Transylvania seven years later, how we went as a group, visiting the castle—standing as it had before but feeling less oppressive now. It had been a trip of catharsis. I stood and watched the sunset behind the castle, the mountains cascading with beautiful colors as the light died behind them. Jonathan urinated on the front gate, his own way of closing the door on history. Arthur set a cross and some wildflowers over the spot where Quincey Morris had died, and Jack and Van Helsing walked the grounds, checking once again that there were no signs that any monsters had returned to the sight. I said a prayer for Lucy, for Mr. Morris, for the crew of the *Demeter*, for the poor women that creature had turned into its demon-brides, monsters with no will of their own, and then I slept the most peacefully I had in all those years, there in a tent on the castle grounds, with Jonathan beside me.

Theodore smiled at me, and Edith, who had been listening by the door, sat in the chair beside me and took my hand.

I told them about the judgement I'd faced in England once Stoker published the book, how the story warped over the years, how some people were even frightened of me because the retelling they'd heard rendered me un-dead, and how I was being further scandalized and portrayed as an adulteress, a harlot, a *victim*. Perhaps that's what I hated the most, being seen as a victim. But the idea that I would betray my husband, that there was anything between the creature and me—that I was anything more to it than a pawn, or it was to me anything more than an oppressor— lives on in my anger. That my son would hear such versions of the story…I prayed he trusted his father and me enough to know our version was the truth. We never lied to him, he knows everything, but who knows what rumors might reach his ears…

I long for a way to reclaim my narrative, I told them. But I am not foolish enough to believe you can fight public perception once an idea gets out.

Having just a couple of people to speak candidly to, however, goes a long way toward feeling like I've reclaimed some of that control.

For a couple years now the Roosevelts, particularly Theodore, have been those people for me. We visit often and speak regularly. We are close to making a real difference in women's voting, I can feel that—maybe a couple years away, provided we get the right politicians elected. Theodore and I swap stories we've collected from others of the strange and eerie. There is no shortage of human atrocities today, especially not in the city, but word reaches us of new legends and creatures from around the country. We talk sometimes about taking our own expedition around the country in search of the hidden beasts.

But lately, my friend is lost in his own head. I know he worries tremendously after Quentin, who is fighting in the war overseas—a pilot of all things, as if there weren't enough to worry about without him in the sky. Theodore often seeks company from someone who knows Quentin as someone more than just the President's son. We don't always talk about his worries, but having someone around who knows seems to help him, and Edith too.

So today, I'm off to Sagamore Hill to spend the afternoon. Theodore sent his car to pick me up from Manhattan, I'll never get used to how quick automobiles have made travel. In no time, I was ushered into the house. Just inside the door is framed needlepoint that asks the visitor: *Leave a little of your happiness when you go*, and even after all this time I can't suppress a shiver when I read it. Edith is away this afternoon, and I am shown directly to Theodore's study. He sits at his desk, a drink in his hand despite the early hour. He greets me as warmly as ever, but there is something behind his smile. Once I'm seated, I see that gravity on his face again. We catch up for a few minutes, sharing what is new in our lives, but I can tell something is on his mind, so finally I ask him.

Taking a deep gulp from his whiskey, Theodore retrieves an envelope from his desk drawer and holds it atop his desk, covering it with his hands. Whatever is concerning him so deeply begins to frighten me, I ponder anxiously what could be within the envelope for what seems like years before he finally speaks.

"Mina," he says, calmly. "I debated upon whether to bring this to your attention or not for some time. I still have friends across the city's police force from my time as Commissioner, and more than one person has shared stories with me…stories that I think may interest you. But I worry might frighten you…"

"Theodore, you've never been shy," I admonish him. "Whatever it is, have faith enough in my strength to share."

Reluctantly he passes me the envelope.

"My boys tell me they've been finding bodies for the past few weeks…all like this." I open the envelope to find a stack of photographs. Crime scene photos. Each one a close-up of a topless body. Men, women, even—my breath catches, my heart breaks as I see—a child. Nothing immediately links the bodies, they are all dissimilar in race, build, in all ways but one. "Each body, according to them, had been drained of blood completely, but not a drop was spilled around the corpse." Which is when my eyes focus on the two pinpricks on each neck, right over the jugular vein.

"Unmistakable. Where were these bodies found?"

"Around Hell's Kitchen." Theodore removes his glasses and settles back in the chair. I, instead, stand and pace with the photos.

"Preying on the working Irish and the homosexual neighborhoods, people the city would ignore. Plenty of traffic from the theatres, but enough privacy in dark alleys. It knows the neighborhood, and its smart."

"Yes, I had the same thought."

"So why did you need me?" The question rolls off my tongue, but I feel I already know the answer. And his expression confirms it.

He rises, walks to me, and presents me with an antique crucifix.

"Something told me you would want to know," he says, meeting my eyes and resting a paw on my shoulder. "I thought you might want to reclaim your narrative."

I think of Van Helsing's letters, all of which are in a box at home. In them, he provided me with years of lore on the vampire, ways of detecting them, every possible way to kill them, likely hunting grounds and resting places, everything I could need should this day ever come. I had hoped it never would, but we both preferred I be prepared. Years ago, I'd even prepared a bag of tools in the case of emergency. Jonathan didn't approve, and even I thought I was being paranoid, but inside I stored holy water, wooden stakes I'd sharpened myself, and Quincey Morris' old Bowie knife. And I am always sure to have garlic flowers at home—I tell myself they're for cooking (I do love garlic), but there might be a deeper reason for it. The bag flashes across my mind as I stare deeper at the photos in my hand.

"Theodore," I meet his eye, burning with intensity, "tell me everything you know."

The night is cold and still in the Kitchen, just beside the theatre district. Streets glimmer from fresh rain, the moisture in the air adds a chill to the atmosphere as I walk, slowly, down West 47th Street. This is not the first street I've walked tonight and is unlikely to be the last. The sun set three hours ago, giving way to autumn moonlight, under which the shadows dance in the streets of a crowded city. The City That Never Sleeps is a perfect home for a vampire, it means an endless supply of victims and enough people that a handful going missing won't raise any alarms. There is one of these creatures in the neighborhood around me. One? Maybe more. Certainly, the number of bodies Theodore told me about could be attributed to two or three. I'll need to find out. This city viewed my story as a fiction, which means it will be unprepared for the real danger of the un-dead. Our hope of preparing the public failed. The vampire's power is indeed rooted in people's unwillingness to believe in it, Van Helsing said that to me once.

Around me stumble all manner of person: the couple eager to get home to their bed, the drunk stumbling his way in what he hopes is the direction home, the theatre-goers oohing and ahhing over the performance that's just let out, a young girl who is clearly new to the city glancing about in every direction, a group of teenage boys looking for mischief. New York is rife with targets. And recruits. Vampirism could spread like a plague in a population this concentrated.

I walk, focused on the task at hand. I can't think about hypotheticals, I can only control so much. Tonight, I look for one. Tomorrow is another night.

As I pass an alley, I hear shuffling and see shadows stir. Pausing, I hear a bottle shatter, followed by what might be a pained whimper. Do I imagine I smell copper? I was once more attuned to that scent; I can't ignore it.

I enter the alley, unsure of what I will find. This might be what I'm looking for, or it might just be another occurrence in New York. From one pocket of my coat, I pull Theodore's crucifix, and from the other I unsheathe a stake.

This is how I continue to reclaim my narrative.

With my wooden dagger held at my side, I embrace the darkness.

My name is Mina Harker. I will be a victim no longer.

Bill Cozza has always drifted to dark literature, and was inspired to start writing after reading *Dracula* at a young age. With a lifelong passion for horror, Bill has a degree in cybersecurity, but his heart is in writing. He is a voracious reader, but never climbs out from under his TBR pile. He lives in Media, Pennsylvania with his wife, cats, and daughter, Mina.

Biting Into Yourself
By R.S. Tiemstra

MINA HARKER'S JOURNAL.

10 February.—Children say the most appalling things. I thought that I would have been long past shocking, given the ghastly experiences of last year, but the cruelty of a young person is, I think, unique within the human species. The girls I am to instruct, all between the ages of fifteen and seventeen, display a downright maniacal imagination towards each other. Such *children* they are!

Yes, I still refer to them as children, though the headmistress and their parents would insist that these are 'young ladies'. As far as I'm concerned, they do not earn *that* title until they leave my instruction.

Which brings me to the matter of Muriel Hill. She's a wispy, distant sort of girl. I fear sometimes that a stray breath of wind will waft her out of my classroom and rid me of an otherwise excellent student. I always knew she was set apart from the other girls, but I never realized how deep the rift was until today.

The words drifted to me from across the yard, as if I was meant to hear them:

"Muriel is a bloodless creature."

A chill arrested me on the spot. I had seen bloodless only too recently. Color leaving the cheeks, bit by bit, until one becomes a ghost. A creeping white death so profound that the blood of three adult men is not enough to bring color back into a woman's cheeks. My dear Lucy, oh, how she faded away…the wisp that remained of her drank, however. She drank deeply.

The voice that had spoken these words belonged to Polly, one of my students. The winter cold keeps the girls close to the schoolhouse, even when eating their lunch at midday. It seemed that Polly had gone to take some air, and had fallen into conversation with Lottie (short for Charlotte).

"She seems a little odd," Lottie said, "But she has always been nice to me."

Polly was already shaking her head.

"A girl like that brings bad luck, you'll see. I read about it recently…A pale, parentless girl arrived in a boarding house in Austria, and by winter everyone under the roof had contracted the fever. They were all dead before the year was out."

"How dreadful!" Lottie's eager tone contradicted her words. She was clearly *desperate* to hear more. But Polly did not elaborate further. She left both her friend and I, her accidental eavesdropper, with our curiosity piqued.

What on earth could cause a girl to say that about one of her peers?

12 February.—Oh, how I wished I could have asked Jonathan for advice in this matter. But Jack and Professor Van Helsing were adamant that he take on no more stress than absolutely necessary. He is not to travel, nor was he to go to lavish parties that could provide undue physical or mental strain (imagine that! Jonathan and parties! They do make me laugh, those two doctors). My worries about the hostility of my gossiping students, I think, would only bring unnecessary stress into his mind, which is already plagued by the worries of the firm, of which he is now sole partner.

I brought the conversation I'd heard to the headmistress, in a casual sort of way, not wanting to cause alarm. Lady Clarke answered my question with an arched eyebrow and the sort of look that one saves for an overexcited puppy. She asked me if that was all I heard. I told her yes, but insisted that it should be cause for concern. She only scoffed.

"Your previous employer told me nothing about these flights of fancy, Mrs. Harker," she said, "Girls gossip about each other. It is only natural."

I realized then that my point of attack had been all wrong. I must have sounded like an intruder into private affairs, rather than someone with real and professional concerns for these girls.

"You are right, Lady Clarke. But since I am responsible for the behavior and decorum of these young ladies, it would not reflect well on my teaching if they started baseless rumors about each other."

If Lady Clarke detected my change of tone, she gave no sign. Pressing on, I added, "Perhaps speaking to the girls' parents might be in order? We want all girls educated here to have first class manners when they leave, do we not?"

I saw a muscle tighten in Lady Clarke's jaw.

"Even if I would sanction such a thing, it would not be possible. Muriel is the daughter of an army Colonel. Like as not, he's in some far-off part of the Empire, doing his duty." She then added, "You would do well to focus on the work—*your* duty is to these children while they are under my roof. You may think of it as a vacation from your dull home life, but for the rest of us, it is a calling."

I knew better than to press the matter.

February 13. Dawn.—I am up early today and cannot return to sleep.

I dreamed last night about his castle. About that place within the Carpathian Mountains. Unlike Jonathan, I've never set foot inside the many rooms in the high towers of Castle Dracula. Though his diary painted a vivid picture of the interior, to me the castle has always been like one of the mountains around it: a tall and solid thing, as old as earth.

In my dream, I crossed that threshold for the first time.

I found it strange—not as my husband described it, but like a large and open cavern, with a ceiling so high it disappeared into darkness. The floor was a pit, through which ran a lattice of thin stone bridges, crossing each other as thickly as a city plan of London. The pathway split and wove and doubled back on itself as far as the eye could see—patterns that made me think of that labyrinth of Minos, where Theseus was thrown to die. I was no Ariadne, and could only watch my own feet carefully and try not to fall.

The stones seemed to echo with a distant scream, and I knew without a doubt that deep below was a young woman. Sometimes, she would flit about in the passages under my feet. I could see her gown, white and ragged all about her. Her arms reached down to her ankles, muscles stretched from some recent struggle.

She was lost here. Running in circles and shrieking endlessly into the dark.

February 13. Afternoon.—I spoke to the girls today, and I fear I have done more harm than good. Either I have lost my touch, or the young women of 1899 are made of sterner stuff than I was at their age.

I took Lottie aside first, under the guise of correcting her handwriting. I hadn't been feeling at all well since this morning, but I swallowed my bile and went to work. The lesson was a straightforward one, but it allowed me some room to press farther. I told Lottie that I had a question for her.

Before I'd even asked, however, Lottie's round face turned a strange dark pink color, and she begged to be excused. I told her she wasn't in trouble, I was just concerned about how my students behave with each other. This only made the matter worse, and she refused to say anything. I must have said something wrong, though I cannot for the life of me think of what.

My interrogation of Polly was longer, but no more successful. Polly was as bold and naturally charming as a girl can be—

someone whom I was certain would marry fast and marry well. But until that time, she was more than happy to direct her considerable charms in…unhelpful directions.

"What can I do for you, Mrs. Harker?"

Polly settled against a windowsill, as daintily as any bird I'd ever seen. I'd learned my lesson with Charlotte—this time, I would be frank.

"It has come to my attention that you've been spreading rumors about the other girls."

The look of innocence was so pure I might have believed it, if not for the many months I'd spent tutoring this girl.

"Me, Mrs. Harker?"

"We do not stand for this kind of behavior. We're here to prepare you for English society, and out there in the real world, gossip has consequences."

There was a glint of defiance in Polly's eyes.

"Does secrecy too have consequences, Mrs. Harker? In the 'real world'?"

This caught me off guard, so I asked her what she meant.

"Oh, you know…when someone is dishonest about their past? Their family? Their whole life? You haven't taught us in our decorum classes what to do if someone is a snake waiting to strike."

"That is an awful thing to say about one of your peers, Miss Clements."

She shrugged.

"I'm looking out for the others, Mrs. Harker. We cannot have a bloodsucker living among us."

That chill again. The blood pounding at my wrist, my temple, my throat.

Muriel does not bleed.

"What did she do to deserve this treatment, Polly?"

The girl considered for a moment before replying.

"It is the way Muriel lingers," she said, "Always watching. Always snooping. She *sticks* on you, like a bad smell. It is something like being haunted."

I did not know how to respond to this, and soon allowed the girl to be excused. Before she left, Polly made one parting remark:

"Why are you still working, Mrs. Harker? Do you not have a rich husband?"

Later.—Jonathan turned in early. His constitution is still recovering, though I fear it shall never quite be the same. In the dwindling light, our small home feels even smaller than ever. I do not believe, even as I write these words, that I am alone here.

I am loath to admit it, but Polly is right. There *is* something about Muriel that sticks to you. Not quite a shadow on the wall, or even a whisper in your ear. But I feel it nonetheless…and it is familiar to me. A lingering presence I have been trying to forget for months.

I had pleaded with Jonathan to let me go back to work when we returned from the Carpathians. I did not *have* to, Jonathan had the money, and the two of us were all too eager to start a family. But I could not be alone at home all day. Not for the time it would take to conceive a child. The quiet would have been suffocating.

Experience has taught me much about the nature of foul spirits.

February 14. Afternoon.—At my request, Muriel stayed in the classroom after the others had gone. She was the same as always: quietly distant, her face still and her eyes slightly misty. I looked up to her, once I had packed away the writing materials from today's lesson.

"You can see the factory smoke from here…"

Her voice was so faint I thought I'd imagined it. Following her gaze to the window, I saw what she meant—a slight brown murk in the clouds, like a smear of mud on a piece of cotton.

"I hope your parents do not mind if you are slightly late tonight, my dear."

Muriel looked away, her head giving a single, quivering shake.

"Is there a problem, Mrs. Harker?"

I told her that I had seen some inconsistencies in her schoolwork lately—a slight exaggeration, but not an outright falsehood—and wanted to know if she was feeling at all distracted lately. Muriel looked up, and though she was looking right at me, I couldn't feel her gaze.

"It is a lot to take in, Miss. The manners, the do's and don'ts…and your less conventional lessons. The languages, shorthand, geography…"

I nodded.

"I understand. It *is* quite a lot to take in. More, I imagine, than your parents will have expected from a private school like ours…"

When I said *parents*, it appeared as if a shudder passed through Muriel. My heart ached for the girl—a father in the army, always away on assignment…no wonder her eyes held such a faraway gaze. She must always be trying to stare over the horizon and see the distant army her father was leading to battle.

Something held me back from probing any farther. I retreated to my role as an instructor, and told her that if there is anything I could do for her, she must come to me first. Anything at all. Her face remained mask-like when she said that she would, and stood to go, adjusting her dress.

That was when I saw it—for just a fraction of a second, so briefly that I was not entirely sure I had seen it at all.

There were two small scars upon her neck.

Later.—My investigation would not end there. It could not. I went immediately for the headmistress's office. There was no sense in trying to persuade her to change her mind. She was determined to stay out of our students' affairs, and when Lady Clarke set her mind to something, she was immovable.

But like all good schoolmasters, she kept impeccably complete records—at least of where the tuition payments came from, if nothing else.

Within her records, I found a small slip of paper with the girl's name on it.

Muriel Hill; daughter of Colonel Arthur and Etta Hill.

Printed below was their address, and I knew it at once. Not far from Eaton Square. A respectable part of town if ever there was one.

That night.—Something resembling a plan has formed in my mind. I will go to their home, introduce myself to whichever guardian is in residence, and prevail upon them the importance of their daughter's social health. Yet even as I consider this, the scars upon her neck hover in my mind. It has not yet been six months since the Count's destruction. Is it possible that some lingering scar could have been left in London by him, or one of his progeny?

If so, I should write The Professor at once. But I can not do so yet—I already know what he would say. *Evidence, dearest Mina. We must approach our problems as scientists, not like a superstitious mob.*

So I will gather more evidence. See for myself what issues this girl faces, in order to determine what help she will need. I've called a coach, and packed some necessary supplies, including the portable electric light and revolver that the professor gave me last year. I thought at first he was silly for letting me keep these things, but now I am grateful. I do not know what I will find at the house of Colonel Hill, but I will go prepared all the same.

February 15th. Dawn—I write this safe in body, but far less so in spirit. I cannot help but think of those words that Shakespeare spoke through Ophelia: *Woe is me, to have seen what I have seen. To see what I see.*

Last night, I did go to the house near Eaton Square. In my deepest fears, I expected a ruin like we had seen at Carfax, a place whose edifice forbade mankind from entering. But this was a fine old place, as elegant as they come in this good old city…it wasn't until the carriage came to a stop that I felt something amiss. The house I confronted was a place without a soul, whose heart had been devoured long ago. The windows I could see were dark and shuttered. Though there was little outwardly wrong with the building, I could sense something of the tomb within its appearance, and I shivered.

My knocking elicited no response. No servant appeared, neither did anyone else. On the third knock, I felt a peculiar sensation. The door was giving way, slowly sliding upon with each successive blow. Inside, there was no light, just murk and dust.

Van Helsing's lamp was enough to push back the dark, but nothing could overpower the smell. It was not like a crypt, or the stink of Jack's madhouse, with its mix of chemical odors and unwashed human flesh. This was the smell of rot—like the worst of the refuse heaps that pile up in London's poorest districts. To think that such a smell could have lain hidden in such a proper neighborhood beggars belief.

I took a step forward, driven not by bravery, but by concern for my student. I could not believe that Muriel lived in such squalor—not the calm, distant girl who listened without listening.

The entrance hall might have been grand, once. Dull gold shone along the edges of the carpet, and gleaming mirrored walls greeted me on either side of the chamber. It was a place made for entertaining, which currently only entertained flies and dust.

I held the professor's revolver before me. My finger did not touch the trigger, for I had no desire to shoot whomever I found within…but its presence reassured me, should I find someone attempting to loot this decrepit place.

Room by room, I explored this old house. The worst of the stench seemed to come from the pantry, where flies and maggots had turned old bread and salted meat into paste.

Where had the servants gone? Was there no one here?

Someone was at home, I would soon learn, though not in the sense that I had maybe hoped. My instincts led me to the master bedroom, where, without fanfare or announcement, I found the lord and lady of this crypt.

They lay abed as if sleeping, but paler than their sheets, their skin the pallor of wet wallpaper. The cold must have kept the insects at bay, but it did little to slow the progress of decay. I surprised myself that I did not scream—for surely I have never seen anything so awful as a married couple dead and rotting in their home.

But of course I have seen such things. I have seen their like in the mind of the Count—his awful fantasies, his many gruesome feasts.

This man and this woman must have been lying here all winter, at least. Could they have been killed while the Count was still in London? It struck me that I never knew the true depths of his appetite…whether there even was an amount of life that could quench his fathomless bloodlust.

I needed to call a constable to this place. I could do no more.

As I turned to go back outside, my light caught on a shadow of pure white.

It was Muriel.

The girl was in her dressing gown, an unlit candle in her hand. She made her way down the stairs toward the entrance hall, as if sleepwalking. She did not react to my light, nor to the gasp I made upon seeing her. I followed her at a distance, holding a handkerchief over my nose and mouth.

It was a strange and terrible thing—the areas she passed through, while clearly showing signs of disuse, were the most well-maintained parts of the house. It was as if this young wraith carved a path of light through this darkness. The mold stopped where her bare feet had tread and the flies kept their distance. Even the dust seemed to part before her. She made her way from her bedroom to the parlor, where she sat unmoving for several long minutes. It was here that I had to do something. I spoke her name, hoping that I could disrupt the oddness of this sight.

Muriel cocked her head, but otherwise did not move.

I said her name again, with a little more of my teacher's authority behind it.

She opened her mouth, but it was not Muriel who responded.

"Miss Murray. I thought that was you knocking at my door."

I slowly walked around Muriel until I could see her face. Her eyes were closed, her mouth hanging open.

"To whom am I speaking?"

The open lips moved.

"Miss Hill, of course."

When it had finished speaking, instead of closing, the mouth dropped open again, as if released by invisible strings. A thin line of drool ran onto her nightgown. Though parts of her would move, there was no tension in her muscles. She might as well have been a rag doll.

"You are not Muriel. Show me your real face."

It murmured for a moment. "You come hunting your own children, Mrs. Harker," the slackened mouth spread in an open, lifeless grin, "Her parents will be concerned."

"What have you done to this girl?"

It rolled Muriel's head, letting her auburn hair fall in a curtain over her face. It was so dirty—how had I not seen this in the classroom? She must not have bathed in months…

"You could have let me be. I will have finished with her before too long. But instead, you took my bait."

Bait?

When it looked up, I could have sworn it had the face of Polly now, and it gave a scornful toss of its hair. The skin was so pale it was almost translucent, and an awful cold light burned from within its skull.

"Decorum does not seem to matter much now, does it, Mrs. Harker? Or are we still concerned with tea cozies and penmanship?"

The neck gave an awful twist and it was the face of Lottie, plump and friendly cheeks now bloated with bile.

"Flesh that has healed is sweetest to me."

I felt a burning at my neck—as if a red-hot pair of tongs was being pressed up against it. The marks where the Count had bitten me, though long since closed up, felt fresh. For a wild moment, I was convinced that I was about to start bleeding freely and I'd never stop until my body was an empty husk. When it laughed I knew these thoughts were not my own. These feelings belonged not to my body but to the thing that wished to possess it.

"Perhaps you thought that when the scars were gone, you would be safe…that the foul things of the night would know you had outlasted him…and they would steer clear, knowing the Mina was not fit to eat."

I raised the pistol. The professor had once said that a sacred bullet might kill a vampire, but what of this? What would it do to a child who spoke with decayed words? Instead of leveling the weapon at that demonic mouth, I turned the barrel toward the ceiling. I fired, and the roar of the weapon filled the room like thunder.

Muriel's eyes opened, and she seemed to shock back in her seat. She screamed and flung herself at me. She was clawing, scratching, howling. The gun went off again, this time as it was forced from my fingers. Hands clawed with desperation forced their way around my throat, where the ghosts of the Count's scars still lay. Yet, the eyes that stared into mine were not a demon's. They were wild, a vivid green shot with blood. They were Muriel's eyes, focused at last.

I tried to speak to her, but my words could not pass my throat. The rotted walls were running, rushing with the dull rust-red of blood, flecked with black spots of mold. We were in an oil painting, my tears reducing the hard reality of this world into pigments and swirls of color.

Then, she released me. Her hands shook.

"What…Mrs. Harker?"

I took her by the hand and led her to the door. The household seemed to roar behind us, pursuing us with a cloud of carrion flies. I could feel it, the bloodless thing, tugging away at me. Every step became a conscious effort—fighting against desire, against will, against my every impulse to stay and disappear into the ground. Muriel and I were stronger together, and each step we took made the next one easier.

I do not remember when it stopped pursuing us, but we'd been long outdoors by then. A night watchman had heard the gunshots and came to investigate, finding a pair of scratched and dirty women, stumbling their way through the night.

I now have in my mind a full picture of events. The Count came to this city in secret, as we all know. Buoyed by his ship of the dead, to enter like a miasma onto the streets of London. While my dear Lucy was the principal subject of his attentions, others fell victim quietly to his more impulsive urges. And in his wake rode not just death, but other damned spirits too. Kin, perhaps, or eager followers of a larger predator. Ever since there have been corpses, there have been maggots.

One of these feasted not on the blood, but on the spirits of victims like this poor girl. The more it ate, the more it could speak her language in hollow mockery, let her sleepwalk to my lessons and lure me in. Where it went after I reclaimed Muriel, I cannot say. It spoke much to me, but told me little of its own nature. I shall make a copy of these pages for the professor. I know not if anything will come of a new investigation, but at least Muriel is safe, and shall return to sanity under Jack's care.

I remember a poem my dear Jonathan once read to me, where a woman unknowingly took a horseback ride with her long-dead husband:

> *Hallo hallo! Away they go,*
> *Unheeding wet or dry.*
> *And horse and rider snort and blow,*
> *And sparking pebbles fly.*
> *Tramp tramp, across the land they sped;*
> *Splash splash, across the sea…*
> *'Hurrah! The dead can ride apace,*
> *Dost fear to ride with me?'*

When Jonathan first traveled to the Carpathians all those months ago, a local had quoted a line from this poem to him as a warning, in its original German. *Denn die Todten reiten schnell.*

The dead travel fast…and seldom do they ride alone.

98

Based in Los Angeles, California, **R.S. Tiemstra** is a writer of fiction, film and audio stories. Their podcast scripts have been produced by Spotify Studios, iHeartRadio, and The NoSleep Podcast, among others. This is their second work on Bram Stoker's Dracula, after co-writing the podcast miniseries *The Real History of Dracula* for Wondery. Their short films as a writer & director have played at over 50 film festivals worldwide. When not spending entire workdays reading about vampire lore, they can be found social dancing, going for long walks in nature, or watching an old movie at one of the dozen or so repertory cinemas near their apartment.

Borne of Woman
A Tale of the Huntsmen
By Dennis K. Crosby

He looked different. Not older, just…different. Facial hair. A scar on his cheek. But the eyes. The intensity. Mina saw nothing in them but darkness. Just as before. He was back now and despite the crowd and her current circumstances, she was not going to let Jack the Ripper get away again.

Mina moved with purpose—her gaze focused on the Ripper. He moved as well, stopping occasionally to acknowledge someone, or excuse himself for bumping into them. How kind.

They were in the Lyceum Theater where a memorial was underway for Sir Henry Irving. Mina had come to know Irving well. He was what she thought the Count could have been, if not for the anger and bloodlust. She couldn't fathom any reason for the Ripper's presence, though. Running into a killer wasn't on her agenda for the evening but given the trajectory of her life to this point, it was more the rule than the exception. Once he was away from the crowd he gradually sped up, until he was finally able to run. Mina moved faster until she reached the hallway, then gave chase.

Through the halls of the upper level, they ran. Mina caught sight of him ducking into a room and she slowed. Cautiously, she walked in and found him standing there. The smug look on his face angered her. As did his tailored suit and hat. He looked like an English gentleman, yet she could feel evil wafting off him like steam from an engine.

"I know you," he said. "Wilhelmina Harker. Wife of Jonathan Harker. Mother of young Quincey."

Mina clenched her fist at the sound of her son's name escaping his lips.

"Your reputation is that of a learned and inquisitive girl. A proper lady. A juxtaposition to your true self?"

The smirk on his face made her clench the other fist. It made her want to do violence. It would have been justified considering what he'd done. For years, Mina Harker and her husband, Jonathan, believed that Jack the Ripper was a vampire—a creature about which they knew a great deal. Years after the death of Count Dracula, a murder echoing the original Ripper killings had taken place, so they decided to investigate. They'd hypothesized that the mutilations had been a cover for the consumption or collection of blood. What better way to throw the police off the scent of the real monster and motive, than to confuse them with unnecessary violence. Their investigation began to bear fruit, and they'd closed in on him in Chelsea. That was when she got her first look at him. But he'd run out the back door of a restaurant and vanished.

Until tonight.

"Tell me, do you fancy yourself a warrior—a hunter—like your husband?"

Don't smirk at me!

"I fancy myself an agent of truth and goodness. A warrior against evil," said Mina through clenched teeth.

"A protector, then?" asked the Ripper, taking a couple of steps forward.

"If needs be," replied Mina, shifting her weight in preparation for defense.

"Is that why you're here? Playing the part of Huntsman. Taking on a role you are ill-equipped to play can only result in a slow, painful, death."

The Ripper removed something from his jacket. A long silver hunting knife that shined brightly despite the dimly lit dressing room.

"Illequipped?"

"Well, the key word in Huntsman is…*man*."

Mina smiled. It spoke volumes.

"That's the problem with you monsters," began Mina, "Always forgetting that man is borne of woman." From a sheath on her back, hidden by a small jacket, Mina drew a stiletto. "And that includes the Huntsmen."

With lightning speed, she thrust the knife forward only to miss the Ripper who ducked to his left. They traded jabs, each missing the other. Mina smiled as she moved. Delighted to be a surprise…but his smirk remained, and it sent her over the edge. She lunged and attempted to find a home for her blade. As she moved, the Ripper side stepped her, grabbed her arm, and shoved her into a shelf. Glass, theater props, and books fell in a whirlwind of chaos. Mina ducked under, covered her head in protection, and felt the Ripper run past her and out of the room.

She collected herself and chased after him again. The dress she wore was custom made to break away. Mina pulled the fabric at the waist as she ran and discarded the outer garment revealing leather pants and boots beneath. Strapped to her left boot, another dagger. Strapped to her right thigh, a custom sheath that held three wooden stakes. Perhaps she would find out tonight if he was a vampire.

Either way, he was going to die.

Mina rounded a corner and saw the Ripper ahead of her. He stopped to look back then quickly faced the door, placed a key into the lock, and turned it. When he opened the door, Mina stopped in her tracks.

That's…impossible.

Beyond the door was a street. And yet, they were on the second floor of the theater. In disbelief, Mina looked at the Ripper who flashed a sinister grin, then laughed. He gave a condescending bow, removed the key from the door, and turned to step over the threshold. Desperate, Mina flung her weapon.

Blade over hilt it sailed with urgency until it struck true in the back of his leg. He screamed in agony, then fell, more than stepped, through the doorway. The heavy key fell from his grasp, onto the floor. Mina ran at full speed. The Ripper reached back and tried to grab the key, but with Mina closing in he grabbed the doorknob and slammed the door shut instead. Frustrated, Mina opened the door and found the Ripper gone. In his place, a storage closet with old costumes and set pieces.

Confusion lay upon her like a heavy blanket. She examined every inch of the closet. No trap doors. No false walls. Nothing. Even if there had been, there was still no explanation for the street she saw.

Did I dream it? Was it an illusion?

Mina stepped back and attempted to process everything. Something beneath her boot caught her attention. She stepped to the side, bent down, and picked up the key the Ripper had dropped. It was strange, not only in appearance, but in feel. It was brass and unnecessarily ornate about the head—a circle, enveloped by two snakes. It was also surprisingly lightweight.

Why were you so desperate for this?

On instinct, Mina closed the closet door. She inserted the key into the lock, turned it, then opened the door again.

Nothing.

What am I missing?

She didn't quite know what she'd hoped to find. Well, that was not entirely true. She'd hoped to find that street. She'd hoped to find the Ripper. Closing the door again, she removed the key, placed it in her pocket, and left. She walked swiftly, anxious to get to the one person in the world who may help her.

The Ripper?! Alone?! Mina!"

Mina lowered her head. Not at being admonished, but because she felt a sense of urgency and had little time for lecture. Abraham Van Helsing was a fine doctor, and in very private circles, a renowned hunter. He was also an expert on the occult, and it was that knowledge that she wanted to tap into. But the filial affection she bore for him begged for her patience.

"Professor," she began, "There was no time to rally the troops. He was there. I had to go after him."

He took a deep breath to calm his own nerves, and her tension eased as well. But the sense of urgency remained.

"Well now, perhaps you and Jonathan can—"

"Jonathan is away with Quincey. He wanted personal time since he'd been gone so much with the Huntsmen."

"Ah, yes," said Abraham. "And that leaves you with this withered old man."

The professor gave a slight chuckle when he spoke the words, but Mina felt certain he'd meant them. She'd been fortunate to have good men in her life. Some, like Van Helsing, had been father figures. Comforting. Patient. In the absence of her own father, and mother for that matter, they'd filled a void that existed for years.

"Does their absence sit well with you?" asked Abraham.

"Oh, yes. Certainly. I mean, I do my best to care for Quincey otherwise, but…a boy needs his father."

"A child needs its parents," said Abraham.

"Of course, professor. I only mean that, there are things he will feel, and experience…as a boy, as a man…that I have no knowledge of. Without the benefit of having grown up with parents to guide me, some things fall to Jonathan."

They both sat with that for a few moments.

"You've done quite well, Mina. Growing up as you did, you've done quite well indeed. Do not allow self-doubt to take refuge in your mind about your ability to mother that boy. Understand?"

Mina nodded.

"Good. Now…tell me more about your encounter tonight."

Mina recounted everything, up to and including the Ripper's disappearance behind a door.

"A street?" asked Van Helsing.

"Yes. I was far away, so I could not make out any landmarks to guide me. It looked as if there was a park beyond it, though. Again, I was more focused on him, I think."

"Indeed. And you said there's a key?"

Mina pulled the key from her coat and placed it on the table between herself and the professor. She looked at it, then at the professor, whose face lost color. Mina was certain she saw him recoil.

"Professor? Are you all right?" she asked.

"I…don't know."

"Do you know this key?"

"I do."

"And it terrifies you?" she asked.

"This key is ancient…and very powerful."

The professor pulled the key closer. He picked it up and studied it as if confirming its authenticity. Mina saw a sense of connection between it and the professor. As if the man had reconnected with an old friend.

"This…is the Key of Ananke," said Van Helsing. "According to orphic lore, she was the sister and consort of Chronos, the personification of time itself. She was mother to the Fates, and goddess of inevitability, necessity, and compulsion. As a primordial deity, she was as responsible for the creation of the universe as any of her generation. This key is said to hold a portion of her power. The power to open pathways through time. Not just the past, but also, to possible futures."

"Surely you don't believe such things?" asked Mina.

"We've killed vampires, werewolves, and demons, my dear. *This* is the thing you choose to be skeptical about?"

Mina shrugged.

"In my travels, I came across such a key," said Van Helsing. "In fact, this very key. It was stolen from me three decades ago by a student I was very fond of. Smart lad. Highly skilled. Such potential. Both he and the key vanished around the same time. Every so often, he'd pop up again. Then just as quickly, he'd be gone."

"Dear god," began Mina, "If the Ripper had this key, he must have taken it from your student. He's…likely dead. I'm so sorry, professor."

A few beats passed.

"Professor?"

"I wouldn't be so certain," said Abraham. "You see, my student's name…was Jack."

Mina's thoughts scattered at the professor's revelation. Her legs lost strength. She hadn't even realized how rapid her breathing was. So many questions. So many thoughts. When she finally looked at Van Helsing she saw a stranger. It took several minutes for clarity to return.

"In all these years, had it ever occurred to you that the killer and your student were one in the same?" she asked.

"Honestly, no. Even with the missing key, and all the evidence, his culpability was never at the forefront of my mind. He was…pure. An innocent if you will. Shy. Inquisitive. I never saw a struggle between righteousness and evil in that boy. Not once."

Van Helsing went silent. He sat. Wearily. Seemingly resigned to the fact that he may have been master to a homicidal apprentice.

"I have to stop him, professor," said Mina, looking down at the key.

Van Helsing, lost in thought, could only nod.

"You said he would vanish, then reappear after some time. It makes sense that he may have gone back to the time you knew him. Do you know where he lived? Did he have family? Friends?"

A heavy sigh followed her questions.

"He was close with another student of mine, William Corcoran. They were more like brothers. Grew up together. Even courted the same woman."

"Woman? Who?" Mina eagerly asked.

"Jane. Jane Westin. Later…Jane Corcoran. Despite that, the boys remained friends, though I suspect Jack was torn. I think he genuinely loved that girl. Even after the marriage…and pregnancy."

Something in his words stirred feelings in Mina. Sadness. Loss.

"The way you speak of them," she began. "What happened?"

"William, equally gifted in medicine, was killed. Jane was there when it happened, and the stress sent her into labor. Unfortunately, she did not survive childbirth. If they'd gotten to her sooner…"

"I'm…so sorry, professor."

"No, no…it's all right. I've long since processed the whole affair. Still, to be faced with it now. And with this key. There's just…"

Mina walked to Van Helsing and knelt. She'd never seen him so forlorn. Was there something more to the story? More questions swirled. So too did that sense of urgency.

"Professor, tell me how to use this. There may never be another chance."

"Mina, no. We must find another way. That key is dangerous. If he indeed went back—things done in the past, changes made, anything even slightly out of the ordinary could reverberate through time and change the present. Everything we've done…everything we've *ever* done…could quickly be undone. Imagine the horrors you could unleash. The horrors you could re-release."

She knew what he meant.

The horror.

Count Dracula.

"You knew him during that time. Where would he have gone? He was wounded. Would he go to a friend? To you?"

Silence answered her back for several moments.

"Perhaps…William," said Van Helsing.

His hesitation gave her pause. Was Jack more to him than just a student?

"How do I get to him? How do I use this?"

When Van Helsing turned to look at her, Mina saw tears welling in his eyes. She recognized them. She'd held tears like that. Many times. They signified guilt. Remorse. They manifested in the knowledge that somehow, some way, you were complicit in death and destruction.

"Professor, I know what you're feeling. But you cannot blame yourself. You didn't know. This is not *your* fault. *He*…is not your fault," said Mina, placing a hand on his arm.

Van Helsing held her gaze, then patted her arm.

"But it is," he said.

Van Helsing rose. Slowly. Mina helped him, then followed him as he walked from the sitting room to his hallway. They both stopped at his front door.

"No. Professor, please. Let me—"

"You take the key and insert it in the lock of a door. Any door. It matters not, so long as there is a lock. Think of where you want to go. A person. A place. A time. You turn once. When you hear the click, you can open the door. Only after the door is open can you safely remove the key."

Their eyes were trained on one another. Even as Van Helsing placed the key in her hands. She opened the front door and stepped outside.

"Stop him," said Van Helsing.

Mina nodded.

The door closed.

She inserted the key.

When Mina opened the door, she saw the same street she'd seen before. She removed the key and stepped through the doorway. A tingle of energy passed through her. In the distance, on the edge of the park across the street, she heard a scream.

"Jack."

Without hesitation, she ran off toward it.

Mina slowed as she reached the area from where the scream seemed to emanate. She was unaccustomed to the area. A nightmare for most warriors.

For Mina Harker, it was just another night.

A rustle in the trees brought her to a complete stop. Mina slowly lifted her leg to retrieve her remaining dagger. Before she could establish herself, a shadow leapt from beyond a nearby bush. His smart dress betrayed any hope of anonymity. It was the Ripper. His limp was gone. In his hand, the weapon she'd hurled at him.

"Harker," he sneered.

His eyes were wide. Frenzied. He was hunched over. Feral. Saliva foamed and dripped from the sides of his mouth. He groaned. Like a ravenous animal. The sight was…

"Familiar," she whispered.

She'd seen that look before. In the crazed patient of Sewards' asylum. A patient under the thrall of Count Dracula. The Ripper was no vampire. He was…a servant to one. Just like…

Renfield!

Fiendish laughter filled the air. The Ripper rubbed Mina's weapon against his thigh, allowing it to cut through his clothing and into his flesh. The Ripper placed the blood-soaked blade against his tongue and lapped up the crimson liquid.

"I…will…be…immortal!" he screamed. "The Master will save me."

The Master? Oh god. No!

Unnerved, but ready, Mina settled into a defensive posture, and then the Ripper struck. Animalistic was the only word to describe the Ripper's attacks. He growled and snarled as he fought. He thrust and swung wildly with her dagger in hand. The speed at which he moved was unholy. Not as fast as a vampire, but it was decidedly faster than any human. Speed compensated for his lack of discernable fighting discipline.

Mina narrowly missed a jab in her abdomen but left herself open to a follow-up attack that sent her to the ground. Her weapon fell from her hand, just out of reach. The Ripper pounced and immediately brought his blade down. Mina blocked his strike with her forearms. His strength was overwhelming. She needed to do something quickly to survive.

"Umph!"

Mina felt his weight leave her and followed the sound. A man tackled the Ripper and the two tumbled over each other.

"Jack! Stop this!" demanded the stranger.

Jack? He knows him.

Mina moved and found her stiletto. She gripped it tightly and turned to join the fray, when just beyond the two men, she saw a woman standing, watching, in horror. At a loss, Mina followed her instinct to join the skirmish, but it ended as soon as she stood.

"Noooooooo!" screamed the woman.

The Ripper managed to roll the stranger onto his back and plunged Mina's knife into his abdomen.

"You…should not…have interfered…William," snarled the Ripper.

William? Corcoran?

With the echo of a woman's cries in her head, Mina snapped. Filled with pure rage she leapt for the Ripper and viciously attacked. She thought of the women he'd killed, and she slashed. She thought of victims that *may* have died at his hands, and she stabbed. She punched. She kicked. *She* was the animal now. But unlike the Ripper, she was well trained. Each blow landed. The business end of her stiletto found its home every time. In the end, the Ripper was a bloody mess on the ground, only a few feet away from the man he'd killed.

"There is darkness in this world, Jack. I have seen it. I have watched it grow and fester on the streets of London and around the world. People think the darkness is in social class or economic standing. But that's not where it is. It's here," said Mina, pointing to her heart. "And it travels even deeper—to the very soul of a person. I have dedicated my life to putting that darkness to rest, using anything and everything at my disposal. You are a scourge on this Earth. Among the worst evil I have ever encountered. And it's time for you to die."

Mina placed the tip of her stiletto against the chest of Jack the Ripper and slowly pushed it into his heart.

Blood spurted from his mouth. He smiled. He laughed.

"The Master sees you. He sees you through me," he said. "He will come for you. One…day…he will…come…"

"I know," said Mina.

Mina fell back. From the ground she saw dots of light above. *Stars?* The word popped into her mind but sounded foreign. Long pieces of wood moved back and forth. There were billowy protrusions along them that moved freely and independently. *Trees? Leaves?* Again, the words sounded strange, yet she was certain they were correct.

Mina.

That was her name, right?

Mina, it's okay. Everything is going to be okay. Just come back.

It was her voice, calling to her, desperately trying to pull her back from the abyss in her mind. Mingled in with the echo of her name, was the crunch of dirt and gravel, and low sobs.

Mina rose slowly and looked over to find a woman next to Jack's victim. *William.* Memories flooded back. *She* flooded back. Finally, she walked over to the woman then knelt next to her.

"I'm…so sorry," she managed to get out.

Looking down, Mina saw the woman's swollen belly. His wife. *Jane?* Pangs of sadness attacked Mina's gut. She knew well the anguish the woman felt. Before she and Jonathan had wed, she thought he was lost forever. It tore her apart. Even after they'd reunited, she'd been concerned for his well-being—both physically and mentally. She was *still* concerned, even after all these years. Perhaps, *especially* after all these years.

"I—"

The woman screamed. Not in agony, but in pain. As soon as the woman's hand went to her stomach, Mina launched into action.

"Okay. You're going to be all right," said Mina, trying her best to be calm, despite the chaos around them. Despite knowing it was the woman's destiny to die. "Let's get you up and out of this park."

"No!" screamed the woman. "William!"

She reached for him. Refused to leave. Mina understood that, too.

"I know," said Mina. "You don't want to leave him. I understand that. But there's nothing we can do for him here."

The woman screamed again and doubled over in pain.

"We need to get you to a doctor," said Mina. "If we don't do that now, his won't be the only life lost tonight."

The screams got louder. Mina did her best not to panic.

"We can't help him. We can help you, though. We can help you and your baby. Don't you think he would want that?"

The grief filled protestations mingled with pain continued for a time. Finally, after falling to her knees a second time, the woman acquiesced.

The screams alerted people nearby, including some Peace Officers. Mina directed them to the scene and somehow managed to deflect obvious suspicions away from her. They'd arrived at a nearby hospital, and after the commotion settled, she was left alone in a waiting area as doctors worked to help the expectant mother.

It was hours before the doctor emerged. He looked like a man who carried the weight of the world on his shoulders. Her heart swelled at the realization that there are so many heroes in the world. Not just those that fight monsters.

"The baby?" asked Mina.

"A healthy girl," he said.

Mina felt her eyes mist.

"And…the mother? Is she all right?"

The doctor took some time to answer. Mina felt her heart begin to pound. Professor Van Helsing spoke of a murdered man named William, and his wife Jane, who died in childbirth. Was this them? Had she been the cause of it all along?

"It was precarious for some time," said the doctor. "She fought hard."

Oh god no!

"Thankfully, she kept fighting. Thankfully, you got her here in time. She is weak. But alive and recovering."

Relief washed over Mina.

And uncertainty.

"When you're ready, you can see her. She asked if you were still here."

"Yes, of course. Thank you."

Mina took some time, steadied herself, then walked to the room pointed out by the doctor before he left. Faint light entered through a window, but it was an otherwise rainy English day. Mina took a seat next to the bed. She found the mother lying there, exhausted, with her newborn by her side. The child looked peaceful, and was, by any definition, a beautiful girl.

"How do you feel?" asked Mina.

A tear fell as the woman tried to answer. Mina knew it was a response to pain, both physical and emotional. This moment, meant to be beautiful, meant to be shared with her husband, was bittersweet. Mina grabbed the woman's hand and gave a gentle squeeze.

"Thank…you," said the woman. It was more of a whisper, no doubt due to low energy and a desire to let her baby sleep. "Thanks to you, I still have a piece of him with me."

Mina gave another gentle squeeze.

"She's beautiful," said Mina. "I am so terribly sorry for what happened."

"No," began the woman, "It's not your fault. Please understand that. Had you not been there, Jack still would have been. And as crazed as he was, my William would likely still be dead. So please, take no blame. You saved lives tonight. Thank you."

The silence was broken by the gentle coos from the baby between them. They both smiled and looked at her. So gentle. So innocent.

"What will you call her?" asked Mina.

"I'm not sure, yet. Oddly enough, William and I never talked about it."

The name again.

"He was…William Corcoran, yes?"

"Yes, that's right."

"And you're Jane?"

"Yes. I'm terribly sorry, have we met before?"

"Oh…no. I'm sorry," said Mina. "I um…just heard the medical staff speak of him, and you."

"Oh. Yes. He worked here. They were fond of him."

"He saved a complete stranger," said Mina. "I have no doubt he was a good man."

Mina stayed a while longer but recognized the fatigue growing in Jane. It was time for her to get back to her own home. Her own family. Her own time. She stood, exchanged more gratitude, condolences, and congratulations—the strange combination was not lost on her—and walked to the door. She stopped at Jane's urging.

"Forgive me. I'm so lost tonight. I don't even ask your name," she said.

"Oh, yes…I'm Wilhelmina."

"It's nice to meet you, Wilhelmina."

"Mina…to my friends."

"Well then it's nice to meet you…Mina."

Mina nodded.

"One more thing," said Jane.

Mina walked back and stood next to the bed. Jane pointed to a silver necklace on the dresser. A Celtic Cross. Mina grabbed it and handed it to Jane.

"I want you to have it," she said.

"Oh dear, no. I couldn't possibly—"

"Please," said Jane. "I insist. It was William's and it would mean a great deal if you would take it."

"You should save it. For your daughter."

"Trust me," began Jane, "she will have plenty of jewelry to choose from."

They shared a quick laugh. Mina stared at the necklace for a bit longer, then put it on.

"Thank you. That's exceedingly kind," said Mina.

It was time to go. She'd done enough. Changed enough. She hoped that she had not damaged the future with her actions. She said goodbye once more and left.

Mina managed to find a quiet area in the hospital and walked to the nearest room with a door. She repeated the steps that got her to this time and place, opened the door, saw her own bedroom, and entered. All was as it had been when she'd left for Sir Henry's memorial. She looked at her reflection in a nearby mirror and saw a haggard woman. Grief and joy blended with harsh battle and death. She wanted to sleep for days upon days, but instead cleaned herself up, changed her clothes, and headed downstairs.

She smelled food as she descended the steps.

Mina stepped into the hallway and was immediately met by young Quincey. He hugged her tightly and asked questions with the speed of a rabbit.

"Easy, easy. Take a breath, son," she said. She looked down at him and felt a flood of emotion. He looked so much like Jonathan. For the first time ever, she wondered if it might be time for them to step back from hunting to make a quality life with Quincey.

She hugged him. And the reciprocation melted her heart.

"How was your time with your father?"

"Good, mum."

"What is he cooking?" she asked.

"Cooking? Dad's not here," said Quincey.

"Not here? Where is he?"

"He's out running an errand."

"An errand? And he left you here alone?"

"Alone? No. Grandmother is here."

"Grand—"

Before Mina could finish, an older woman rounded the corner. Mina gasped. She knew her. Immediately. She had lines at the corners of her eyes. Her hair was slightly grayed. But her smile was the same. Her warmth. Her image became blurred as Mina put the pieces together.

"Hello, sweetheart. Are you hungry? I've got—"

Mina's mother put her hands to her mouth. Her eyes shifted rapidly from Mina's face to the Celtic Cross necklace she now wore. Awareness filled the room. Recognition.

"It *was* you. I've been waiting for this day. All these years, I've watched you grow into this woman. My savior. My friend. My…sweet girl."

"J-J-Jane?" whispered Mina. "Mother?"

"I think we have some catching up to do," said Jane, walking forward. She touched the necklace she'd given Mina all those years ago.

"I guess you finally decided on a name," said Mina.

The two shared a laugh, a cry, and a hug. Then, with a bewildered Quincey in tow, they walked to the kitchen for breakfast…and a history lesson.

Dennis K. Crosby is the award-winning author of the Kassidy Simmons series. Since 2020, he has published three urban fantasy novels and fourteen short stories in the horror and supernatural thriller genres, including *Weird Tales Magazine #370*. Dennis holds a Master's Degree in Forensic Psychology and a Master of Fine Arts Degree in Creative Writing. With experience in retail sales, private investigation, and social service, Dennis uses his knowledge and experience to craft compelling characters experiencing real world challenges against the backdrop of magical, supernatural, and mythological phenomena. He's been the subject of several interviews and podcasts, a guest speaker at multiple conferences, Co-Chair of the Horror Writers Association's StokerCon 2024 in San Diego, and a panelist at both WonderCon and Comic-Con International.

Dennis grew up in Oak Park, IL, and currently makes his home in San Diego, CA.

The Black Dog of Hampstead
By Macoy Greco

LETTER, MINA HARKER TO LUCY WESTENRA.
(Unopened by her.)

12 April.

My dearest Lucy,—

It has been two years, and I still cannot keep from writing you. Although I have the sense to avoid penning these letters anywhere but beside your tomb—for I should otherwise deliver as many as would flood the mausoleum—your name haunts my diary. All my pen-strokes merely shadows, etching the white of your silhouette.

Always, I long to ask after you, and ache as you cannot answer. My only solace is detailing to you my happenings. Mundane though they've become, I fear filling the stationery with every thought in my mind. For this, you must forgive me. I am uncertain if your spirit is permitted to access my journal, and I cannot always visit.

I thought I'd find no occasion until Summer, having to account for fifty students atop my regular class—and administrative duties. These are so tiresome I shall not write of them. My presence owes to the "extended" Easter holiday. I'd forgotten it, until finding my students astir, packing to return to families and all-important debutante balls.

But I must speak about the girls, Lucy! It's hard to believe you and I were ever so lively. Or, rather, that I was. You never lost it, not even when engaged to Arthur. Constantly they are whispering, and covetously petting each other, as we would. They are fond of those practical jokes you enjoyed playing, always sweetly, and I without the will to discipline them. Even in school, a girl must have the freedom to play, to twine unfamiliar hair between her fingers, laughing until her face is red and buried against the grass—if not her schoolmate's skirt. Despite that each receives admonishments, I hope all enjoy, without trepidation, their festivities—although I doubt any are as beautiful as you, Lucy, on your debut.

I fear for my girls, seeking to learn amid our shroud of propriety. The girl whom the schoolmistress deems my worst student, I merit my best. She has little aptitude for etiquette (which, you recall, is all we teach), yet she is voracious. I've begun tutoring her in academic subjects, assigning additional literature papers to keep her apace with her marks. Still, I can't forget the look in that poor child's eyes as she left for home. I, who'd taken her trust, was forced to meet them, to somehow reassure her, while her father's cane tapped, and she flashed with new understanding of the world she would inhabit. I suspect she's not the only bright spot in England darkened too early. There must be many whose eyes are not permitted to shine with the same sadness.

You must forgive my tirading, for lately I engorge upon the New Woman writers. Whatever can be said of girls, balls, and the world writ large, one simply cannot deny the sun's pleasantness in spring. I feared today would be overcast, leaving me little opportunity to recall how sundrops nestled in your curving skin. If I am to visit you in death, I should prefer it be overmastered by the specter of life. Oh, but mind the careless associations of my words, I'm sure any thought of dark powers is lamentable to you. Yet, I had an odd encounter on my way to the cemetery. My most striking in some time.

Bluntly, the Hampstead sky had been brushed across with clouds. Dense as gravestones, depressing even a pleasant mood.

The only consolation was their purposelessness, for I was certain it would not rain. Two voices barked back and forth. One belonged to a thin, doctoral man. He was on the defensive, his wiry, articulate voice knocked about the thunder of his opponent's—a butcher, by the meat shop behind him.

"A great, black dog! Nothin' else! Jaws wider than the heath!"

"Dear god, next you shall say it dragged clattering chains—"

"It did!"

And so forth. The mention of the black dog stirred dreadful curiosity—Whitby seems so long ago—so I asked the source of the commotion. The doctor gestured to his companion, whose smile was wolfish, as he began:

"It happed Thursday evenin'. When fair-'aired little Mary Graysmith, freshly engaged, turned up missing after takin' a moon-light wander 'cross the heath. None knew what caused it, 'til findin' her fiancé at the family 'ouse, all covered in bites and blood. The maid saw a big, black dog, prowling at the edge o' her lantern light..."

"Or an escaped wolf." The other chimed in. The butcher glared.

"She says it vanished, into smoke and shadow. And I know it wasn't no wolf. 'Cause I seen it."

He seemed expectant for some gasp or yelp. But my heart was overburdened with worry. I lent him a nod, hoping it would sustain him.

"Long past eleven, I was lockin' up for the night. About to put away my beauties—" He glanced, obviously, toward the hanging meats. "But my juiciest loin 'ad disappeared. That's when I 'ear all slobbering, and chomping, and–" he elbowed the doctor, "—rattlin' chains, and see it gobbled by the biggest dog I ever saw. It was blacker than coal, with terrible, red eyes—"

At last, I gasped. Overcome by a thought I had done all to keep at bay. Those eyes!

Seeing my unease, the men made to console me. I re-gathered myself, asking about the fiancé.

"I visited the lad," the doctor recalled, "His wounds exceeded me, but the family consults a specialist in bacteriology—the name, Romanian, escapes me. The paper has it."

Would you believe newsboys still swarm Hampstead? Even on our street, one shouted away: "Black Dog terrorizes Hampstead! Wilde on trial!"

As I thanked them for their time, the butcher took it on himself to hurry over and purchase a copy for me, altogether refusing repayment. How constantly I am reminded of man's good nature, in a world overfull with evil. I was so touched, that I have avoided the article like death until now.

But, Lucy, stay close to me. At a glance, the newsprint induces nausea. The picture of the doctor—an alleged expert in wolves—with his aquiline nose. Then Mary, whose sweetness shines, even from her picture. Her hair curves lazily around her bare neck.

God, this poor girl! If it truly is him, Lucy! Him, who we know surely is dead. Who, in the caverns of my mind I must always suspect and await—some investigation must be made. For her sake, ignoring humanity's, I cannot hesitate. No matter how my throat throbs with ill memories.

I intend to devote this weekend—to the last hour—to uncovering the truth of this "black dog." Certainly, Jonathan cannot mind my saddling him with Quincey (for his health surely forbids his involvement). But I shall write to you on that later, for it begins to rain. Wish me luck, I promise to visit soon.

Your loving,
Mina.

"The Westminster Gazette." 12 April
'BLACK' HOUND HAUNTS HAMPSTEAD.
GIRL GONE MISSING.
(Pasted in Mina Harker's Journal)

Long regarded as an ill-omen by country-dwellers, and a staple of signage by pubkeepers, a black dog, like that described in tales of "Black Shuck," has made several startling appearances in the neighborhood of Hampstead.

Much of the commotion surrounds the disappearance of 19-year-old Mary Graysmith. Graysmith, and fiancé Philip Ward, were reported missing after failing to return from a walk. Later that night, the family's maid discovered Mr. Ward unconscious, ravaged by bite and claw marks—believed to be inflicted by a black dog she alleges seeing near the home's steps.

Ward, still comatose, receives treatment at the Graysmith family estate, placed under the care of Doctor Andrei Vernescu, Romanian microbiologist and cynologist. Mr. Graysmith was quoted saying: "We pray for his recovery and hope he may shed light on this utter damnation."

Already, outlandish theories circulate about the missing girl, in conjunction with speculation on the dog's origins—which many suggest are satanic. Dr. Vernescu was quick to dismiss them, remarking: "It is a wolf. Perhaps some wild hound, nothing more. In England, you say we easterners are prone to superstition, but I find the belief your own preoccupation with panic. Much can be said of my countrymen, but they, at least, have accepted their ghosts."

Still, sightings abound, the creature described by several Hampstead residents, including a butcher, a barmaid—"Sign of the times it is!"—and the maid who initially spotted it. Though her testimony was nearly unintelligible, due to lingering terror, the creature's description remains identical in all cases: black fur, red eyes, and, occasionally, rattling chains. Police are instructed to watch for stray dogs, and already the keeper of a Hampstead pub has been spotted repainting his sign. The paint, our source tells us, was black.

Letter, Mina Harker to Lucy Westenra.
(Unopened by her.)

12 April-Evening.

My dearest Lucy,—

I cast sense aside, writing you from the comfort of home, though the word rings falsely.

You would love our current dwelling, for the architecture inspires romance. Yet, it is rather spacious for three. We have tried to make it a comfort, and it's horrid to complain about something so gracious—inherited from dear Mr. Hawkins. However, when alone in the foyer, only able to converse with the rain's oppressive pattering—you needn't imagine why I write.

But, you were always impatient, wishing for good news straight away, so I shall say I have confirmed an appointment with the Graysmith estate, at ten tomorrow. I hope they can forgive my lying about an association with the Exeter-News-Letter (still, I play at being a lady journalist). For some causes, the truth is worth bending.

I have only ever been completely honest with my diary, with you, of course, dear, and to Jonathan. This policy, I have never regretted—but, Lucy, I told him all over dinner, and it lay terribly. For the longest, he refused to acknowledge me, instead commenting on the haddock, or the rain, or else swirled his wine around his glass.

His head was bowed, so his hair shone silver against the candlelight. I suspect this was to prevent me from seeing him blanch at each mention of the hound. You must understand I could not relent. He grew whiter than I have seen him in some time, even amid his illness—for his vitality comes in waves, rotting always beneath his work. Even when returned…I fear he relinquished some part of his strength, delivering the last strike by Kukri.

Still, as I declared my intentions, he was resolute. His jaw bulging outward, he told me:

"Mina, I forbid you."

I could scarcely believe it. I laughed, for it was sweet, in its way.

"Mina, I mean this. I cannot let my wife pursue devils, nor stray dogs. You must understand, I am master of the house—"

"Master?" It was vile to hear that word from his mouth. "Jonathan, you are my husband, not my jailkeeper."

"By law, I am both."

"Not law, custom. But it's meaningless. You have said yourself, this evil is beyond modernity—beyond nature! Someone must act, and we both know you…" I quieted.

"That, we do." His voice shuddered. I cannot say whether with fear, anger, or even love. "Perhaps this occurrence warrants inspection by one of our band. Someone acquainted with his signs…" He reddened altogether, a shock against his white hair. "I can't understand why that must be you! Summon Arthur! Seward! Christ, Mina, even Van Helsing would not hesitate in coming from Amsterdam! After all that was done to you, why —?"

"Jonathan, only you and I know his effect. In our blood, we know. And I so much the worse that I cannot ask another to go in my stead. They have wives who depend upon them, children —"

"As do you!" His roar frightened me, for he never yells. "You have a son! You're a woman, Mina! My wife! I allow you to work, but you cannot go pretending it is not so!"

He fell, fatigued, in his chair.

"Besides, it might be nothing, you would waste your time. I prefer optimism in lingering matters of Count Dracula." He attempted to let the name fly, indifferently. But I heard his tongue spasm over it, as if he'd cut it upon his teeth.

"Then, there is little harm in investigation."

"Save the train fare, my love."

How often we're teased for our strange play between warmth and coldness—you, Lucy, were something of a recidivist—for we are both of cerebral inclination. Now our temperature seemed misaligned entirely, placing warmth in pleasantries, to hide coldness in our hearts. His next words chilled me altogether, saying, without looking: "Mina, I have no power to hold you. But, as you go, I cannot promise our marriage shall follow."

He fled, leaving me to stew upon his words. I know he will forgive me, but should he not…God, Lucy, how terrible was the evil that passed us, to rob me of the two I have loved most. It claws at me from beyond its grave, and Jonathan, as ever, finds no immunity. I hate to hurt him, yet I cannot close my eyes without seeing that poor, innocent girl. I realize I've torn you from your peace as well, invoking you so incessantly, love. Do not think me selfish for it.

The rain, battering the window, returns more memories. Omens I should have read sooner. Jonathan thinks my pursuit naive, but it was I who compiled our records. I, who shared the vampire's mind. This danger, I know well enough to choose. For Jonathan's sake too, Lucy, and—oh, Quincey cries. I marvel he was not woken sooner.

Your loving,
Mina.

Letter, Mina Harker to Lucy Westenra.
(Unopened by her.)

13 April.

My dearest Lucy,—

I rose early, recovering sleep on the train. The sight of London–and the boroughs we once frequented—is bittersweet.

Ten o' clock nears, but fret not for my punctuality. I received a telegram delaying my visit to noon. This, I'd hoped to avoid, for our foe is then permitted to change his shape, and I have every wish to deprive him of advantage.

Alas, maddening myself with paranoia does no good, for I've brought as many of the old weapons as I could, excepting rifles— we do not keep them. If suitable supplies might be purchased, I shall augment my capabilities in the city—but I feel the train slow.

Your loving,
Mina.

Letter, Mina Harker to Lucy Westenra.
(Unopened by her.)

13 April-Later.

My dearest Lucy,—

By mischance, I arrived early, abandoned to a drawing room. I sense a woman's hand in the arrangement, but it is nothing to pry at, for Mr. Graysmith—a kind-seeming old man—greeted me alone.

Amid warm furnishings, my leather case festers gloomily. It contains those necessities Van Helsing has prescribed: sanctified bullets, flasks of holy water, wooden stakes, etc. Only, it is lacking one silver cross, for that is around my neck. As well, I left Jonathan's knife. It felt wicked to use in spite of him. Instead, I patronized a gun shop in Hampstead.

While I imagine Quincey—your Quincey, who I hope entertains you well—would appreciate the walls of rifles, and an overwhelming animal musk, my attention was entirely upon a mounted doe. Her eyes shone with delicate fear.

Attempting to peruse, I found myself facing a dozen near-identical rifles. My confusion must have been obvious, for a voice, accented, asked from behind:

"You're driven to hunt, madame?"

Not recognizing the voice, I replied, "I am to try foxhunting."

I turned, finding the doctor from the newspaper: Andrei Vernescu.

Any resemblances were lessened in the flesh, though not nonexistent. He must have sensed recognition, for he asked if we had met. I said we hadn't, but revealed my appointment.

"Ah, Harker. The journalist." He smiled, knowingly. "Foxes are not your quarry. That rifle will suit you best." In one, unbending movement, he pointed, remarking: "We have wolves in Romania." How could I ever forget?

He pronounced he would deliver me to the estate, unless I had another appointment. I was choiceless but to assent. He then walked to the store's mouth, and, from there, watched me. I confirmed his selection with the clerk, and decided upon a lovely little knife—antique, with a silver handle, and thin, tri-angled point. It is already a comfort to have at my side. What a strange figure Dr. Vernescu is, for I am certain he is not Dracula—how

could he be? Yet, I am uneasy in his presence. I dread to think—
or even to write—it, but might he be another of that kind? A vam
—He knocks. I am sure it is him. Guard me, Lucy.

Your loving,

Mina

Letter, Mina Harker to Lucy Westenra.
(Unopened by her.)

My dearest Lucy,—

Though the pen hangs in my hand, duty remains to document all I have seen…

"Apologies for delaying, Mrs. Harker." The cloak of Dr. Vernescu billowed as he entered. "Mr. Graysmith grew tired. He cannot answer questions." He paused, for objection, then continued: "It is better, for he has little involvement with this omen, and we must not aid his unrest." He bid me to rise.

"Of course." I followed obediently down the hallway. "Would you clarify the nature of your encounter? The Westminster Gazette reported you had not seen it directly."

"Ah. One must keep apprised of competitors." His eyes seemed to search me, as if peering into my deception. "Yes, I have not seen this animal. However, I may show you hairs collected from Mr. Ward's clothing, and his bite marks. The teeth bear no natural comparison, a fact certain to shock your readership."

His cloak swept from behind him, gliding into the parlor as we entered. Its tip seemed to point, theatrically, toward the shivering maid, nearly entombed in her leather seat. She looked purely pitiable in her distress.

"Doctor," I began, unable to draw my attention from her. "What do you make of supernatural speculations?" I'm sure he followed my gaze. The sight lent his words a graveness.

"Since you have read the gazette, you are acquainted with my beliefs. Should these incidents be brought to light, their truth would hold little lasting interest. Be gentle with Mrs. Fowley. Her health is poor."

I scarcely noted his response before he vanished. An adjacent door slammed. I shuddered with the start. The maid was too raddled to notice. Stepping forward cautiously, to avoid startling her, I observed how her wrinkles, marks of gaiety, were malformed by sunken bags beneath her eyes. I feared she had not slept in days.

"Mrs. Fowley? Shall I fetch you something to drink?" She did not respond, concentrated on a habitual muttering—saying, I think: "no crying, miss, he's a fine man." I repeated the question, louder.

With effort, she turned. I gasped, for her eyes were like a lunatic's. She reached for me.

"Miss," Her tone wavered. "don't trouble yourself, that's my responsibility…" I took her hand, worried she would lose the sudden vigor.

"Stay with me, dear. I need only ask a few questions."

"Certainly, Miss…"

"Harker. Mina Harker."

"How lovely."

I could see her exertion. With guilt, I broached upon the dog. She inhaled, sharply, her grip loosening. I held firm.

"Please, your encounter. Then I may release you."

"Master Ward. On the steps. He…reached for me." The poor soul shuddered. "It…bayed! Awful! Every breath! I…"

"What did you see? What sort of animal?"

She clutched my shoulder.

"Blood!" She cried. "Phillip's blood!" Weeping openly, her tears mingled with drool.

"A trail." She shuddered. "Across the cobblestones. Look! It stains my carpet."

The phrase confused me, then I watched her finger rise, toward the door. I hadn't noticed it open. Flooding through the doorway, swirling into the carpet's patterns, was a pool of blood.

The baying that wrung out forced a shiver down my spine. Once my wits returned, I hurled myself blindly toward the noise, fearing the worst.

I must have looked heroic, storming through the doorway with my rifle in hand. However, I cannot feel the savior, for bent over the bed—at the mouth of the lolling blood—was the black dog. It ate from the stomach of Philip Ward.

How horrible the tearing and snarling, like a terrier with a bone. It scoffed intestines, lapping greedily after the blood—going so far as to lick clean the bent-open ribcage.

Amid the carnal display, I could somewhat make it out. Its face was like a wolf's, only snub-nosed. Its eyes closed with pleasure, snout glistening joyfully—coated freshly in red.

I did not hesitate long before firing. The first several sanctified rounds merely startled it. As one cut across its flesh—it seemed justice to see it bleed—its red eyes opened, reaching for me. They burned with pain, altogether too human. But they were not Dracula's.

Half-frozen, I worked tremblingly to reload. The monster stalked toward me, then seemingly changed its mind. It scrambled from bed to desk, leaping out the window. As the thrill in my chest subsided, I realized the glass had not been crashed through, but was already shattered upon my entrance. Then, I heard gasping.

His cloak mangled beneath him, Dr. Vernescu lay against a bookcase. Three gashes tore across his arm. I crouched beside him.

"Mrs. Harker." He said, nearly conscious. "I was wrong. God forgive me." Shuddering, he reached for my cross.

"As was I, my friend." I placed it in his hand, vanquishing any suspicion of vampirism.

"What will you tell the News-Letter?"

"I'm not all I've said." I laughed and, with my knife, cut a piece from his cloak. I tied it tightly around the wound.

Placing a pillow beneath his head, I swore to return by nightfall, and set out after the black dog. Or such was my ambition; the streets confounded me—you always played guide in Hampstead. After some fruitless hours, I write, hoping it will jog something. Alas, I should regroup at the manor, dark will have fallen by my return. There is a newsgirl, perhaps she can provide directions. Although she seems frightened…

…Lucy, how fortunate I was! The girl spoke rapidly. Even I could not record her exactly, but you shall have the tenor:

"How d'you do, miss? Or ma'am? Or whatever's proper. You ought to know you can't be outside! The papers aren't fibbin'. A dog's about! I sawed it!"

Asking her its course, my purpose betrayed me.

"You're madder than a wretch, miss! Would you shake hands with Tom's ghost?"

"If I must. Please, would you tell me?"

"Okay! I watched it run onto the heath, past the cemetery —" I quickly shushed her. The mother in me wished to hug the frail, excited thing. I settled for sending her with a few shillings.

With little time to waste, I acquired a hansom to the manor —how expensive hackneys are now, and I but a schoolteacher. I write from the backseat in an uncertain mood. What luck! What terror!

For, my Lucy, I shall be visiting your grave again.

Your loving,

Mina.

Letter, Mina Harker to Lucy Westenra.
(Unopened by her.)

13 April-Evening.

My dearest Lucy,—

The veil of mist clung to our carriage as we neared, ever closer, to the heath. I marked our progress by the rising church. Loudly, its bells tolled. Dr. Vernescu bent forward, praying. A cross hung around his throat. Watching him—and recalling Mrs. Fowley—I understood why Jonathan, and the rest, had insisted on keeping me from darkness. Little as it helped, in the end.

"Doctor," I said, as his prayer finished, "If I ask too much—"

"No. My obstinance damned us. Denying so plain an omen. This vukodlak." He spat it.

"I am familiar with vampires." I confessed to his shock. While his questions were many, I quieted them. "All you must know, is they are like death. Once one sets upon prey…there is nothing you could have done. It could only have been delayed, and, failing that—"

The carriage stopped beneath us. Dr. Vernescu nodded, for my meaning was understood.

I can only imagine the terror of Arthur, et al., on their sojourns into Kingstead cemetery—and not only for thought of your plight. The fog was thick enough to part the headstones, concealing anything beneath the knees. The moon, in the last hours of fullness, hid behind the lancing spire of St George's parish. Its shadow fell atop the graveyard, conjoining the surrounding trees into one mass. I shone my lantern into the open mausoleums, fearful the light would catch upon two red eyes.

Avoiding thorns, we crept beneath the trees. Reaching, at the church's outskirts, a withered gate, half-sunken into the earth. The wrought-iron doors were torn open. Beyond this portal, lay the heath. Its ponds shone in the moonlight, ever more spectral beneath streaming mist. This, converged from either side in a heavy fog, until all was obscured from view. I distinguished Dr. Vernescu only by his lantern's faint glow.

Yet, before my sight filled with swirling, milky opal, I watched a dark shape beside the water. Its neck twisted skyward, into a snubbed lupine snout. Wild howls tore the shrouded air. My fingers nearly slipped from my lantern's handle. Somewhere beside me, I heard a crash.

"Doctor!" I called.

"I am here, Mrs. Harker!" I turned, having sworn the voice came from the opposite direction.

My lantern forced aside the fog, aided by rays of moonlight. Racing forward, grateful to see the uneven ground, I perceived a figure, still uncertain. For a moment, it seemed human. The beginnings of "Doctor!" leapt from my throat—until two red eyes flashed into my sight.

The pupils curled hatefully. I readied my rifle. As the bullet flashed from the chamber, clouds passed over the moon, darkening all beneath. Still, I heard the growling breath upon the wind. I could not tell from which direction.

A rush was in my breast, for every turning of the mist, every shift in the howling midnight breeze, chanced to be the demon I sought—or it that sought me! God help me, I knew not whether I was hunter or hunted.

Each tongue of fog lapped at my sanity. I cannot say what force caused me to endure. In the haze, under my lantern's glow, I swore I could see apparitions. Jonathan's silver hair, urging me to turn back. The whites of your dress, Lucy. Your lily hand, guiding me forward, toward yet more figures of women, dear Mary's, embattled by the dark smoke. Your pale hair fell about my eyes.

Then I felt the darkness thicken, and a black shape plunged toward me. I nearly shrieked, but it was only a branch. Turning again, I gasped in earnest, for an obsidian snout prodded my cheek.

This, belonged to the statue of a horse, mounted on a worn stone base. I was in another graveyard. It could not have been yours, dearest, but it did me good to tread near death, for I knew you would be close beside me.

My lantern lit upon a plaque, revealing the name: "St. Mary's."

"Oh, Mina, like at Whitby!" I nearly heard you whisper. I simply nodded, for tears welled in my eyes. At my ears, the wind whistled, as if you were behind, quieting me. Whisps curled across my cheek, to wipe the tears away.

"Hush, Mina." By God, I heard you say "Mina." The dancing mist curled into your smile, coy and light. You blew a kiss that nipped at my ear, sweeping through the shrouded fog.

Then, the very air opened before me, parting to reveal graves, sloping up a rising hill. A curdling shriek rent out, halfway between a dog's yowl, and a girl's cry. As it resounded, the moon burned through the clouds, fiery in its fullness—or nearly, for it was shadowed enough to be a waning gibbous. The light revealed, atop the hill: the vukodlak. Risen, anthropoid, onto two legs.

It had not noticed me, so I took aim. My finger was upon the trigger, when I realized it lay in the throes of some horrific paroxysm. Howling toward the moon, its limbs thinned. Splayed pink fingers tore from heavy claws. Golden hair whipped along its matted neck. The red seeped out of its eyes. Then, all at once, its coat of fur fell away, leaving only the pallid, shivering figure of a woman.

The moonlight overmastered her form, casting her in shades of gossamer, even as the shadows assayed to conceal her. On either side of the heath, London's buildings stood sharply, like the teeth of great jaws poised to devour her whole.

She turned, seeing me. Her eyes gleamed with terrible understanding. My heart was glass, shattering under the weight of this poor girl's plight—so like yours, dear, yet so unlike it.

"Mary! Mary Graysmith!" I called, drawing off my coat, making a show of placing it upon a grave—for the night was drafty, and I feared for her health.

I called a third time, but she seemed to be in a daze, making no reply. She turned back and stumbled away. Swallowed altogether by the mist.

Forgive me, Lucy. This is all I can write before sleep takes me.

Your loving,
Mina

Letter, Mina Harker to Lucy Westenra.
(Unopened by her.)

14 April.

My dearest, Lucy—

It is morning. Light warms my skin. I am again by your grave, for I could not be kept away.

Last night, I stayed in a spare room of the Graysmith home. It broke my heart to tell Mr. Graysmith about Philip, and the death eats at Dr. Vernescu. He is well, only scratched, and viciously frightened. I have recommended him and Mrs. Fowley both to Dr. Seward's care and shall telegram Dr. Van Helsing as soon as I am home.

I have told none the truth of Mary Graysmith. Instead, explaining the "vampire" fled to its coffin, becoming dust upon my slaying it. I think Dr. Vernescu suspects, for he remarked, as I left: "Vukodlak, Mrs. Harker, means not only vampire…"

Nonetheless, Lucy, Mary's affliction shall be our secret, and my mystery to solve. I see no reason to subject her to another manhunt, when I might cure her quietly, before the moon waxes.

And, my dearest, I cannot say if, somehow, you aided me from beyond this last night, or if the mere thought of you so ameliorated me. No matter the truth, thank you, Lucy.

I should be leaving, for Exeter, in hopes of repairing my troubles with Jonathan. But I would like to sit with you a little while longer.

Your loving,

Mina

Macoy Greco is a current Writing & Literature student in the College of Creative Studies at the University of California, Santa Barbara. She enjoys writing comic books, pulp, and anything pre-modern. You can find her comic work at www.macoygreco.com.

Willy

By Doris V. Sutherland

Did you meet Grady's parents?"

It was Fae's first question after Parents' Evening. The staffroom fell silent as everyone awaited my reply.

"Yes."

"And did you bring it up, Bella?"

"I mentioned his interest in Victoriana."

"And they were *pleasantly surprised*." Fae's words were deadpan, her glare shallow.

"I suppose so."

"Bella, they have no idea what's been going on in school. Someone has to tell them."

That's when I stood up to face her. "Why? This stuff's not hurting anyone, and I get along fine teaching them."

"Teaching who?"

I realised my slip. "Grady, I mean Grady."

"Grady's not a *they*, though, is he? He arrived a boy, he wears a boy's uniform, and his pronouns are obvious. Tell me you're not humouring this nonsense."

"Sometimes you've got to humour kids."

"When they're calling *Roblox* an artistic accomplishment, not when they're denying basic reality."

And that was it. Iron curtain down, conversation over. As always, silence fell when the conversation turned to Grady.

Grady was a quiet kid who spoke when spoken to and gave good answers. His best subject was history, and his interest was genuine.

Then he started claiming to be a Victorian lady.

It began when he turned up for KS3 history with a pencil sketch, very accomplished given his age, of a familiar-looking building. I asked if it was the abbey.

He replied with a nod. "The ruin of Whitby Abbey, which was sacked by the Danes, and which is the scene of the part of *Marimion*, where the girl was built up into the wall."

(I knew *Marmion* was a Walter Scott poem. I had no idea it was on the English syllabus, though.)

"It is a most noble ruin," he'd continued, "of immense size, and full of beautiful and romantic bits; there is a legend that a white lady is seen in one of the windows."

I had to shoot warning glances at a few sniggering kids before turning back to Grady.

"And you drew it yourself?"

He nodded again. I didn't know which department to commend the most: English or Art.

After that, it was rare for a week to pass without at least one odd moment from Grady. One time I asked the class about historical sites they'd visited, and Grady chose the abbey, of course. He told us how he'd lost track of time there, hanging around the ruin for a few minutes and finding hours had gone. This was how he prefaced his story: "what I have to tell you is so queer that you must not laugh at me." Naturally, the others *did* laugh at him, the only twelve-year-old who didn't realise "queer" had shifted meaning.

The point of no return came when Grady handed in an essay on the Magna Carta. The research was solid, as I'd expected from him. What gave me pause was the writing style: eloquent in an antiquated way, not just grown-up but old-fashioned. I was suspicious he'd copied it from a book or used ChatGPT, but there was another wrinkle. It wasn't just Grady's writing style that'd changed, it was his handwriting. The whole essay had been penned in a sweeping cursive.

At the bottom was a signature bearing the name Wilhelmina Harker.

I brought it up to my partner Zoe. She'd been busy on a long-term archeological project in Chester, but called practically every hour I wasn't working or sleeping (and I loved her for it).

"Perhaps he got someone to write it for him," she suggested.

"Then his ghostwriter put an awful lot of effort into sounding like *anything but* a twelve-year-old boy. They didn't even sign with his name."

I called Grady to my office. He looked rather prim, his hands clasped at his waist.

"Well, the research is solid," I told him. "You always were a good pupil."

"You praise me too much, and…" He swallowed before finishing. "And you do not know me."

I held up the paper and pointed to the signature. "I know you well enough to know your name's Grady Weaver, not Wilhelmina Harker."

"I have been since yesterday in a sort of fever of doubt," he said.

He was talking the same way he was writing, and it took me a second to comprehend his reply. "Why, what happened yesterday?"

He glanced side-to-side and lowered his voice.

"You must be kind to me, and not think me foolish that I have even half believed some very strange things."

If this were an act, he should've been working with the Royal Shakespeare Company.

Before I could figure out a reply, he spoke up. "I can show it to you if you like."

"Show me what?"

He reached into his pocket and handed me a sheet of neatly-folded paper. I opened it to reveal yet more cursive handwriting.

"By all means—read it over," he said.

The bottom line of the letter, behind the *I-am-anxious-and-it-soothes-me-to-express-myself-here* talk, was that Grady Weaver believed himself to be the reincarnation of a woman who lived at the turn of the century.

Every week, conversation bubbled up in the staff room only to be squashed. *He needs a therapist* was countered with *it's not our business.* Each *he's causing a disruption* would go up against *it's just a phase, let him sort himself out.* Every *we should tell his parents* would run straight into *but it's hardly a safeguarding concern.*

I could barely talk to Fae without the argument reigniting. I reminded her that we sometimes had kids from religious families, who came to doubt their faiths or even switched religion altogether. We never told their parents about that.

"That's different," she said.

"Why?" I asked. "If he believes he's reincarnated, that's a spiritual matter."

She held up her hands. "You win, I suppose."

That settled things for the short term. But we still needed to settle things in the long run, and I had an idea to help move things along.

Okay," I said to my class. "Some of you might remember what March the sixth meant back at primary school: World Book Day!"

I'd hoped for a round of misty-eyed nostalgia, but most of the kids looked blank. One tittered. Oh well.

"As you may have heard," I continued, "this school's decided to start celebrating World Book Day. We'll have a book-swap station and an optional reading challenge. We're also going to have some fun with dressing-up."

The titters and eye-rolls were spreading.

"Sure, I know what you're all thinking. Turning up dressed as Captain Underpants would be *so* primary school, right? So here's a couple of things. One, it's not mandatory, you don't need to take part if you think it's silly. Two, we know you've all moved beyond your favourite picture book. If you like reading about science, then maybe you could dress as Einstein or Marie Curie or even a hydrogen atom."

Then came the time for the trick that always worked: slip into a casual demeanor, smile subtly but sincerely, and frame myself as the sort of teacher they find *unironically* cool.

"And perhaps my history lessons will inspire you to become a Reformation person, or a World War II soldier, or whatever. Okay, class dismissed!"

As the kids departed, I was pleased to hear a few snatches of conversation including the phrases *Tudor bloke* and *WAAF uniform*. Before long I was on my break, which meant one thing: a phone call from Zoe.

We chatted about the Roman villa her group was unearthing, after which she asked if I'd made the big announcement.

"Yup! I thought the higher-ups were mad when they suggested World Book Day for a bunch of—y'know—*newly-cynical* secondary schoolers, but those kids might go along."

"Even the dressing-up thing?"

There was something I hadn't mentioned to my pupils: dressing-up had been my idea.

My colleagues had taken a lot of convincing. They said our students were too old; I pointed out that even middle-aged people do Halloween these days. Some of my colleagues had primary school-aged children of their own, and didn't see World Book Day in terms of homespun creativity. To them, it was a grim business of picking the mass-produced skin of some character from Roald Dahl or Dr. Seuss or Kayleigh Raven (you know, those people who'd gone past *children's author* and ended up as *brand* or *franchise*). They envisioned hordes of Grinches or Scholomance Smiffy clones stomping about our school, but I pointed out that kids with no time for something fancy could settle for a cheapo plastic Viking helmet.

"Some of them seem kind of enthusiastic," I told Zoe.

"And Grady…?"

Only Zoe and I knew the whole truth: it was for Grady's sake alone that I insisted on costumes. I hoped it'd let him get this reincarnation stuff out of his system, even if that meant turning up at school dressed as a Victorian lady.

"We'll see about Grady. But yeah, I'm guessing he'll pick Wilhelmina Harker for a costume."

"Uh-huh. Who the hell *is* Wilhelmina Harker, anyway?"

"She's just—" I began, and then realised something. I'd assumed Wilhelmina existed entirely in Grady's mind.

It'd never occurred to me that she might have been a real person.

The library was built from glass and brutalism and looked right onto Whitby Abbey. Past and present side-by-side, making the perfect place for school trips. I'd tell every new class that the abbey was where the Synod of Whitby took place in AD 664, when the local church decided to align certain tenets with Rome—including the date of Easter. Glazed-over eyes would light up when the pieces fell together. People who lived here nearly a millennium-and-a-half ago decided when we modernites should eat our chocolate eggs.

"Hello, Bella! Checking out the local history?"

I'd long been on first-name terms with the entire staff. This was Emma, whose big round glasses made her look like a cartoon caricature of a librarian.

"Heya, Ems. I'm looking up someone who might've lived nearby in Victorian times. Her name was Wilhelmina Harker."

She tapped her chin, repeating the name as though it rang a bell. "Oh, yeah, Mina Harker! We've got some of her papers."

It felt surreal to hear someone other than Grady talking about Wilhelmina as though she were an actual person. "Wait, you mean she was someone important?"

"Hold on, I'll show you the special collections."

I followed her past cabinets of microfilm and shelves of leatherbound almanacs. She unlocked a door labelled *Authorised Persons Only* and led me into a narrow corridor.

"Mina Harker's one of the people covered in the…" (she twirled a finger as she tried to remember the name) "…*The Golden Dawn Collection*, that's it, from an old magical group. One of its members bequeathed some of its resources to us."

Whitby attracted lots of Gothy types, so that tracked, but I was curious to know more. "What sort of magical group?"

"That Victorian stuff with ghosts and seances. I think it was a secret society, although our donor apparently didn't agree. Anyway, there you go."

She pointed to the uppermost shelf, which had a ring-binder labelled *Harker Documents*. I pulled it out and flipped through. Inside, housed in plastic sheets, were pages upon pages of typewritten documents. The name Mina Murray jumped out again and again, before being replaced by Mina Harker. One paper looked different from the rest, like a professional publication. It was an essay by someone called Ármin Vámbéry, entitled "The Scholomance Legend in Romania."

"Oh yeah," said Emma, looking over my shoulder. "Apparently Kayleigh Raven came here when she was writing *Scholomance Smiffy*. Before my time, though."

The essay said something about the Scholomance being a school in the mountains of Romania, where the Devil himself taught black magic to his pupils. Then my eye fell on a book that'd been behind the ring binder, a shiny modern paperback called *Reincarnation*. I took it out and opened it on a page that'd been bookmarked. The section was about historical figures who believed in reincarnation:

According to the writing of Professor Abraham Van Helsing, the turn-of-the-century authoress, adventuress and occultist Wilhelmina Harker was fascinated by the notion of reincarnation and frequently discussed it with colleagues. Rumours persist that she believed herself to have been, in a past life, a bride to Vlad III of Wallachia; however, this assertion went unrecorded prior to 1992 and remains unsubstantiated.

There was more. I saw Three old notebooks had names on their wrappers: Dr. John Seward, Jonathan Harker, Mina Harker.

"Just so you know, you're only supposed to be here for a half-hour," said Emma.

By that point, I'd already opened Mina's notebook.

I was disappointed by the lack of historical figures about school on World Book Day. There were comic-book superheroes, manga heroines in outrageous wigs and a few vampires. Even the knights in plastic armour looked like they were from some fantasy novel.

Fae and I had a pleasant chat, trying to identify characters from our own childhoods. All the while, I was steeling myself to broach *that* subject.

"I've been looking into local history," I said. "Turns out there really *was* a Wilhelmina Harker. She lived through the turn of the century."

Fae deflated at the Grady Matter entering conversation. "Coincidence. Name was probably common as muck back then."

"I don't know, she seems right up Grady's alley. She believed in reincarnation and past lives. She honestly thought she'd met an actual *vampire*. She collected legends about black magic from the Scholomance."

"Hold on, what? The *Scholomance Smiffy* books are just kids' stories."

I made the hand-wave dismissal that always worked on pupils who got history from Hollywood. "I've never read *Scholomance Smiffy*, all I know about Kayleigh Raven is that she got rich and then went off the deep end when she discovered social media."

"Kayleigh Raven speaks the truth, Bella. She's one of the bravest—"

"This isn't about Kayleigh Raven, alright? The Scholomance school is an actual Transylvanian legend, the real Wilhelmina Harker knew about it, and now Grady somehow knows an awful lot about Wilhelmina Harker."

"You're not saying he's *right* about being a reincarnation?"

"No, I just think—"

I was saved from finishing my sentence when a costumed kid dashed past, bumping into me. Fae yelled an admonishment, our conversation forgotten.

The costume was familiar. I'd seen variations on it all day. Pupils milling around in black robes and white masks, or white robes and black masks. Cardboard masks, papier mâché masks, all with dents for eyes and mouths, harsh countours for cheeks and noses, and formations that might've been hair, or judges' wigs, or Tutankhamun headdresses. Children hidden inside weird spooks from some jumbled chess-set.

A couple more flittered down the hall. "What *are* those black-and-white characters?" I asked Fae.

"Wow, you really haven't read *Scholomance Smiffy*, have you? They're the Solomonari, the dark-magic tutors."

Our conversation was interrupted again, this time by a chorus of jeers. I hurried around the corner to investigate.

That's when I saw Grady.

Since he first mentioned it, I'd familiarised myself with that Walter Scott poem he'd mentioned. Call it getting down with the kids. One character, Constance de Beverly, is a novice nun who masquerades as a pageboy to be with her lover, Sir Marmion. While she's in disguise, someone pulls off her headgear to reveal long, golden, girly hair. As punishment for abandoning her vows, she's walled up in Whitby Abbey.

Grady was dressed as Constance de Beverly. He was wearing a medieval pageboy costume, all filthy and tattered and topped off with a long blonde joke-shop wig. What really caught everyone's attention, though, was the make-up. He may have thought himself a Victorian, but he was clearly familiar with YouTube face paint tutorials. His Constance had sallow cheeks and grey bags under her eyes, while her fingernails were stained with red as though she'd clawed out of her cell.

A bunch of guffawing kids clustered around him as he headed down the corridor. Some had their phones out, filming him. One boy yelled out *Willy*, and others repeated it. Then someone shouted *Queer* and the chant became *Queer Willy*.

Fae and I gave some strong words. The crowd departed, grinning kids scattering in all directions.

"If they share those videos," said Fae, "we'll be in the shit."

SCHOOL "ENCOURAGED OUR SON TO IDENTIFY AS VICTORIAN WOMAN"

Two Whitby parents were outraged to find that their son had been allowed to wear a wig, adopt the name "Wilhelmina" and identify as a woman born in the nineteenth century while at school. Frank and Simone Weaver allege that their son, Grady, 12, was encouraged by staff for weeks or even months before they were informed.

I showed the headline to Fae.

"Yes, Bella, I told Grady's parents. Someone had to."

"For God's sake, didn't you think for a second about—"

"Your career? Don't worry, I didn't name you."

"Fae, that's not what I—"

She interrupted again. "I'm not blaming one person, I'm blaming the entire bloody school. I signed up so I could *teach*, not indulge stupid fantasies. So yes, Bella, rest assured that it's not your job on the line here."

WHITBY TEACHER SUSPENDED IN REINCARNATION ROW

A Year 8 teacher has been suspended after objecting to a male pupil reportedly being allowed to identify as a

Victorian woman. Without the school's permission, Fae Taberham informed the parents of Grady Weaver, 12, that their son was using the name "Wilhelmina Murray" and claiming to have lived in the nineteenth century. She has asserted that, after her every attempt to address the matter internally was blocked, her only remaining option was an external disclosure. The school has identified this as a breach of protocol regarding the personal information of pupils.

I was reading the report when, right on schedule, Zoe phoned.

"Have you read the tweets about your school?"

Oh, God. I hadn't read a single "tweet" since they were rechristened "X posts."

"Why, what are people saying?"

"Bloody hell, Bella, it's not just *people*. It's Kayleigh Raven."

What? Call still open, I loaded my browser until I found it. I assumed It was a fake at first, a Photoshop job. But no, what I was seeing was a post by *the* Kayleigh Raven.

KAYLEIGH RAVEN WEIGHS IN ON
"VICTORIAN LADY" SCHOOLBOY SCANDAL

Scholomance Smiffy author Kayleigh Raven has commented on the controversy over Grady Weaver, the 12-year-old Whitby schoolboy who began identifying as a Victorian woman.

"My heart is scalded by this ever-spreading blight of the spirit," said Raven in an X.com post. "That the pillars of learning could so corrupt innocence is testament to our epoch's decadence."

Raven's new book, *The Illustrated Secrets of the Solomonari*, is scheduled to be published next month.

"It's like she's everywhere," said Zoe. "I can't get away from that woman."

I could only agree. I was still seeing those black-and-white Solomonari outfits, long after World Book Day, and worn by people too tall to be schoolchildren.

I changed the subject and got Zoe chatting about that Roman villa.

And then Grady went missing.

His tearful parents were on the news, describing the afternoon when he never returned from school. We all figured he'd run away, but nobody had a clue where to.

The school was blamed. The news avoided mentioning us beyond token references to the boy-who-thinks-he's-a-Victorian-lady controversy, but social media named names. Our inboxes filled with hatred that evolved into threats.

After Fae's suspension, Grady went from a touchy subject to a staffroom taboo as we waited for some sort of update. Every time Zoe called, I'd relish and cherish the opportunity to open up. I'd talk about deliciously mundane topics like the scourge of ChatGPT, while she'd enthuse about the mosaics in that villa ("They'll be big news soon!").

I visited Whitby library on a regular basis, asking every staff-member if they'd seen Grady. Finally, after she was back from a break, I spoke to Emma.

"I don't remember him coming in at all," she said.

I'd tried not to get my hopes up, but even so, I was surprised by the finality of the answer. Grady seemed such a bookish boy: between the YA novels and the Victorian biographies, I would've thought he'd find the library a heaven on Earth. And that's even before we get to the special collection guest-starring his past self. Those were my thoughts while I chatted with Emma. She brought up all the tabloids and online talking-heads and told me what they'd been saying about Grady's disappearance.

"Don't tell me," I said. "Kayleigh Raven's been mouthing off again."

"No, that's the thing. She hasn't."

"Busy with her book launch?"

"It's not that, either! She's cancelled all her public appearances. Her PR department's putting out vague excuses. It's like she's vanished."

The cloud's silver lining, maybe. I chided myself for such a nasty thought.

"I see her fans are still about, though," Emma continued.

She was looking out the window at Whitby Abbey. I saw what she was talking about: a couple of figures among the ruin, gone in a flash, dressed in black and white. More of those Solomonari.

That was when my brain made a connection. Grady's drawing of the ruin. His costume. The poem about the girl trapped in the abbey. It seemed a stretch. But it was a connection that only I could make, I was sure of that, and so I was obliged to make it—for Grady's sake.

Emma looked concerned as I dashed for the exit.

Something about my surroundings bothered me as I neared the abbey. I heard the wind blowing, birds singing, and my own trudging footsteps, but nothing else. The city-sounds, the revving cars and distant yells, had disappeared.

I carried on until they stepped out. Black-robed Solomonari appeared from the shadows, their white-robed brethren emerging from behind ruined walls. Not schoolkids in cosplay but the real thing, their masks carved with the aesthetic remnants of some long-forgotten culture.

"Where's Grady?" I called out.

As one, they pointed upwards, and I craned my neck.

Another white-robed, black-masked figure was above me. I could see the robe's bottom, the boots' soles. The person seemed to be—but that didn't make sense—

No. "I'm looking for a missing child, I've got no time for stupid tricks!"

The levitating woman laughed. Rather than the cackle of a storybook witch, she laughed the way my co-workers did if one of my jokes happened to land.

"You accuse me of a levitation trick." Her voice was soft, feminine and familiar. "How hopelessly muddled. You're trapped in an illusion, but not a conjurer's performance. What you *see* is the abbey as it now exists; where you *stand* is the abbey of centuries ago."

"You're gibbering."

"Are you unfamiliar with the Synod of Whitby? An event that shaped the calendar of our whole society happened right here. Which makes this place a wellspring of temporal magic."

My body went chill, my brain into overdrive. It was making sense, nonsensically. That was why I could see but not hear the city's traffic. The masked woman was standing on the upper floor of the abbey's central tower, even though it'd long been lost to time.

If I ran, where would I end up? Modern-day Whitby? Somewhere in history? Out of existence?

Whether I liked it or not, I could only watch as the sorceress stood and removed her mask. I recognised her visage from TV interviews, back-cover author photos, online reports about social media controversies. Her presence seemed absurd, as though I'd stepped into a pop-art collage where Kayleigh Raven's face had been pasted onto a reconstructed druid ritual, yet it also felt an inevitability.

"When I was a child, a dusty old book of legends told me of the Scholomance," said Raven. "Reading those words, I felt as though I could smell every aroma and see every colour of that school. Knowing it to be more than mere fable, I sought out any scrap of information I could find."

She began walking through the air, her body lowering with each step as though she were descending a staircase long since destroyed.

"That was how I discovered Mina Harker. I visited Whitby and read her writing in the library. I felt kinship with her. Her description of her encounter with that dark, beautiful man who'd graduated the Scholomance made me feel as though I'd known him as well."

Her clack-clack-clacking footsteps halted.

"I swear Mina watched over my shoulder when I wrote my stories about the Scholomance, helping to ensure that the legend and its magic yet lived. But where did that kinship with Mina come from?"

I noticed the Solomonari bowing their heads like a congregation at prayer.

"I concluded that Mina and myself must be one. I was her reincarnation, just as she was the reincarnation of the Impaler's bride. I was destined to wield the Scholomance's key. Then that *boy* came along."

Raven moved her arms in the air, as though pushing apart a pair of upright slabs. That was when Grady emerged from whatever weird camouflage concealed him. He was levitating, like Raven, but on his back—squirming, writhing, desperate to escape.

"Grady!"

I wanted him to reply, I yearned for him to say something, even if it was only *queer* or *hotch-pot* or *a haandbaaag*, just so I'd know that he was still Grady, the quirkiest boy in the school, and this was all some smoke-mirror-hologram prank.

Raven yelled a nonsensical incantation and I felt my throat contract. I could barely breathe, let alone call again.

She carried on talking. "Naturally, he ran to the abbey, a place in which to escape his own time. My faithful and I were waiting for him."

She put her hand on something clasped to her belt. It was a dagger, fashioned in the Bronze Age manner, which she held above Grady. Above his heart.

"A small temporal rite shall correct history's accident. Mina's soul shall be born into *my* body, not his."

She began chanting in what sounded like Latin, and yet unlike any Latin I knew. I wanted to scream, to interrupt those foul words spewing from Raven's mouth, to break the spell she wove over Grady. My throat strained, my jaws ached, but not so much as a choke could come forth.

Then my pocket vibrated and I heard a buzz. My phone! Evidently, whatever weird magic was splitting time hadn't severed *every* connection to my own era. Could I speak, I would've bellowed my gratitude.

I pulled the phone from my pocket and pressed "answer."

Zoe skipped introductions. "Bella, you won't believe this!"

I set it to speaker and pushed the volume to full blast.

"The mosaic is Constantine the Great! Or maybe a Biblical figure, we're not sure. Just wait 'til I can share the photos!"

I pointed the phone at Kayleigh Raven. Her face contorted as she tried to concentrate on her fine-spun webs of syllables and intonations, as though the merest inflection could tear apart her spell, while Zoe nattered about Romano-British aesthetics. God, I loved that girl.

Kayleigh Raven stammered. She stuttered and spluttered and her words came unthreaded. She tried to regain her incantations' rhythm, but it was too late. The Solomonari's masks did nothing to hide their fear as the abbey began *changing*. The past flashed into view: I glimpsed completed brickwork replacing broken ruins, a flagstone floor segueing into green grass. Blue day and black night flickered across the sky. The masked figures scattered in all directions, fleeing whatever fate awaited those who stayed.

I needed to run, too. But Raven still clutched her knife, poised to thrust it into Grady's flesh out of sheer rage.

So I ran to him. I didn't need to see the spiral stairs to navigate them. I stumbled, but reached the top in time to shove Raven's knife-arm. The blade spun from her grip and clattered below as she lost her balance. She tottered backwards, straight for the high window that looked out upon a chaotic day-night sky.

Busy gathering Grady in my arms, I didn't see what happened to Raven. I merely heard a scream that cut off in shrill distortion.

Sheer adrenaline carried me down unseeable stairs while holding Grady. I stopped for a second to set him on the ground below.

"You'll be fine!" The sentence came out as a single, garbled word, but at least I could speak again.

Hand-in-hand, we kept running. The houses, cars and roads of Whitby were in sight. When we grew close enough to hear the traffic, I risked looking over my shoulder and I saw the same ruined abbey I'd seen every day since moving here. Then Grady collapsed on the glass.

I turned to find him sprawled on his back. I screamed his name and knelt down, taking him in my hands.

His eyes were open. He was out of breath but smiling.

"Fortunately," he said, "I am not now of a fainting disposition."

Despite everything, I laughed.

K ayleigh Raven's disappearance was international news. It'd be misleading to say she was *never seen again*, though. Looking through local archives, I found repeated references to that woman in white being glimpsed in Whitby Abbey over the centuries, across time. Standing silent, or wailing in torment. Whenever I pass the ruin, a shudder runs through my bones.

The Weavers moved out of Whitby soon afterwards. Can't say I blame them, although I hope the parents learnt to understand their child in the end. I'll never forget the last thing that kid said to me, right after the ordeal at the abbey.

"The world seems full of good men—even if there *are* monsters in it."

The comment seemed a little sexist, but I let that slide. Wilhelmina's a girl of her times, after all.

Doris V. Sutherland is a UK-based author who has already done her bit to expand upon Bram Stoker's fiction with *Midnight Widows*, a creator-owned comic about the further exploits of Dracula's three brides. Her other fiction includes licensed tie-ins for the television series *Doctor Who*, *Survivors* and *The Omega Factor*. Her non-fiction writing has been published by Liverpool University Press, Obverse Books, *Amazing Stories*, 2000AD.com, *Belladonna Magazine* and the multi-Eisner Award-winning Women Write About Comics, where she serves as Books Editor.

The Harrow Letters
By Lindy Ryan

In the ashes of the Harrow's End wildfire, among charred bones and broken china, we found these pages—scorched, but not silenced. They speak of a woman long forgotten by the world and perhaps by history itself.

A woman once named Mina.

Whether these are the ramblings of a deluded recluse, or the final testament of a cursed woman remains uncertain. What remains is this: a voice, enduring, persistent, reaching out across time from the embers of ruin.

June 3, 2025.—The cicadas hum so loudly tonight that the sound seeps through the very cracks of the house—rising up between the dry rot of the wood, clinging to the old walls like mist. I sit at the kitchen table, my hand trembling as I write. My veins shine blue beneath my papery skin. The lantern flickers. I catch sight of my reflection in the dust-caked windowpane.

A horror.

The sharpness of my bones has become a cruel architecture. My nose juts thin and pointed, my cheeks gone so hollow they might collapse inward so that I swallow myself whole. My legs, frail and sinewed, resemble those of the scrawny chickens that peck at the dirt in the garden. It is as if my body wishes to become a single fang: ready to pierce the world one final time.

Long so—so long ago—I might have passed for a woman in her prime. Now I am withered, a corpse exhumed and set upright in its best dress in a mockery of the living. Yet, even diminished, even shriveled, my heart beats. Slowly. Reluctantly.

My condition was never completed, only begun. Only abandoned.

Once, long ago—so long ago—my name was Mina. I was a teacher, a bride, and—for a time—a heroine. Now I am nothing, a nobody no one remembers as Adeline Harrow. A pale shadow stitched into the fabric of this forsaken Texas land, scattered with mailboxes and a feed store as run-down and dilapidated as I.

The air tastes faintly of ash, though there's no smoke. Not yet.

They call this place Harrow's End, and it is a fitting end, indeed. Most folks left years ago when the rains dripped dry, and the soil cracked like old pottery.

But I remain, because I must.

June 7, 2025.—Each dawn is harder. The light peels my skin, drives burn into my bones. The morning bruises me even through the shutters and heavy drapes. The heat sucks at my skin like breath. It hasn't rained in weeks, maybe months. The grass in the field snaps beneath my feet.

They say fire follows drought.

I remember the night he came. I was twenty-three. Beautiful, they said—like a field of wildflowers before the harvest.

He was a man of foreign manner, foreign name. Years have passed, decades, a century, and I have not forgotten his name, but neither will I speak it. Even to write it seems reckless. Dangerous.

He came to our farmhouse door with promises of salvation from the cholera that swept through the countryside. Desperate to save me after my fever took a bad turn, my husband welcomed him in.

The fever broke, true enough. But so did something else within me.

I did not die.

But nor did I remain truly alive. When the doctor bled the foreigner dry and drove the stake home, they said the evil had passed. That I had been spared. But evil doesn't pass. It lingers—like rot.

Like me.

June 15, 2025.—A bat roosts in the attic now. Each night it flutters through the rafters, its shrill cries no different from my own frustrated whimpers. Perhaps it senses me as one of its kind.

Perhaps not.

I do not feast on blood as the legends claim. The taint runs subtler through me. I wither and rot and decay and yet do not perish. Not vampyr, not revenant, not ghoul. Something unfinished. A seed that never blossomed, left to corrode beneath my skin.

Hunger gnaws at me, but food tastes of ash.

To stave the worst hunger—the clawing, mind-sundering, agonizing need—I've taken to consuming only liquids. Thin soups, broth from chicken bones and boiled weeds and bitter herbs gathered from the cracked fields that no longer yield any harvest. I pretend this is for health, for delicacy. Yet each time I sip, a secret delight coils in my chest. The viscosity, warm and clinging to my tongue, too much like blood to not please me.

Too much like blood to not torment me.

When the townsfolk still come to call, they leave offerings on my porch. Fresh bread. Preserves. Even the occasional chicken. I accept their gifts with polite gratitude, though I have no need for them.

From each chicken I take the bones, clean and polish them, and add them to my collection. What is not boiled into broth is strung along the edges of my property. On the stoop. From the eaves. These garlands of death clatter when the wind blows. It is an invitation, an offering to whatever might finally come to claim me.

A dinner bell, of sorts, for whatever else hungers in the dark as I do.

July 2, 2025.—The journal before this one is missing. Perhaps I left it by the old oak tree out in the east field, where I sometimes sit and pretend to pray. Or perhaps the wind claimed it. The fields are as unkind to paper and memory as they are to seed and soil.

Sometimes I think the earth itself resents my presence. That the fault is mine that the rains have abandoned this place. Even this land, harsh and wild as it is, does not want me as its own. There's a tension in the soil now, as if the earth is bracing for something.

It holds its breath like I do: waiting for the match to strike.

When I tend what's left of the dying garden, the plants shrivel faster where my shadow passes. Even the crows avoid me. Even the ants.

But I persist, alone as ever.

Once, long ago—so long ago—a black cat adopted me. She lasted a year before vanishing into the night, hissing with her fur and hackles raised. Perhaps she too realized that death itself skirts around me, unwilling to touch me.

I do not blame it.

July 16, 2025.—My mind drifts more now. Memories surface unbidden: the scent of my first husband's hair, the way the wheat bowed before a summer storm, the sound of hymns on a Sunday morning. All faded.

I remember the taste of Jonathan's blood, though I never meant to take it.

In my thirst after the fever, in the first wild confusion, I bit down on his hand as he wiped my brow. It was just a drop. A tiny thing.

But enough.

Like our crops, he withered within a month.

Jonathan would have forgiven me. I believe that still. He believed in salvation, even for the damned.

Still, I fled before the others noticed. I left behind the gravestones of my kin, of my dreams. Only this land accepted me again, decades later, when no one remembered my face. When everyone I once knew had been planted beneath the dry, ruined earth.

They thought, then, that when the one who bit me perished before the evil fully took hold, I would be freed. For many years, I believed it too. But you don't save someone by leaving them half-alive.

I lived, I married again. Baked bread. Buried friends.

They always feared what I might become. No one ever feared what I already was.

But now, as death closes in, I feel the pull—the dark thread in my blood tightening, calling me home to something far older, far crueler than life.

August 1, 2025.—Tonight, I saw a figure at the edge of the field.

Tall. Thin. Wearing a wide-brimmed hat.

Watching.

The field blurred at his back—wavy, like heat rising from pavement. But there is no pavement here. Just scorched grass too dry to even remember the taste of rain. Perhaps the figure brings the fire with him.

The figure did not approach, did not call out. It merely stood there, patient as the grave. The one who made me is long dead, but dead things don't stay buried. Not when they leave something behind.

Perhaps it is not him, but a messenger. Perhaps it is the summons.

If he comes again, I will not run.

I will not beg.

I have lived too long for shame.

August 4, 2025.—No sign of the watcher. But the cattle down the road—what starved pitiful few remain—were found dead. Drained white.

Not my work. I swear it.

I have lived these decades resisting the hunger.

My curse is not one of thirst, but of stasis. I exist in a state of decay without end, and in my worst moments, I envy the creatures who can simply die. Be done.

But even now, part of me clings to the world.

And still the heat rises. The shutters warp from the sun's torch. The air inside the house shimmers. If I were truly dead, would I still sweat? Would I still dread the crackle in the distance?

Once, my words helped slay a monster. They called my journal a map, a light in the dark. Now, even the shadows ignore me. I tend the empty garden from which no one will eat. I sew quilts no one will sleep beneath. I write letters no one will read.

If that isn't hope, I don't know what is.

August 20, 2025.—The wind smells of smoke tonight. Not the sharp scent of hearth fire or cookstove, but something deeper —dirtier. Wildfires creep closer from the west. I can see the glow on the horizon, a false dawn that stains the sky with its own kind of hunger.

What's left of the chickens refuse to leave the coop this morning. The bat didn't stir. Even the wind feels afraid.

If fire claims me, will it free me? Or simply reduce me to another smudge of ash even the wind forgets? He once carried boxes of earth across oceans to sleep. I can't even find peace in my own soil.

I leave this journal here on the table, should anyone find it. Should anyone care.

August 21, 2025.—I dreamed last night. I have not dreamed in a hundred years.

Jonathan stood before me—young, strong, smiling. Just as he looked before we crossed into that cursed land.

His hand reached for mine. But when I grasped it, his flesh crumbled into dust.

Then there was Lucy—my dearest, sweet Lucy. Radiant as the moon, her eyes wide with sorrow. But she turned away before I could speak. She always does.

I woke weeping, dry and croaking. Like a woman whittled from old wood.

The bat in the attic cried out too, as if mourning with me. Perhaps it dreams of fire, too. Of smoke curling through the rafters and taking us both.

We are kindred in our sorrow.

September 1, 2025.—It is time. The sky has turned the color of blood oranges.

I have taken the old shotgun from above the mantle. It is rusted nearly useless, the shells too light for comfort, but perhaps it is enough.

I will walk to the edge of the field where the watcher stood. I will wait.

If he comes, I will go with him.

If he does not, I will find a way to end this cursed half-life at last.

September 2, 2025.—Dawn again.

No figure.

Only the wide, empty Texas sky and the endless, whispering dirt.

And me.

September 5, 2025.—I have buried the shotgun by the oak tree.

I am not ready.

The body rots, but the heart clings. And even half-alive, some part of me refuses still to surrender.

The fire still comes, slow and sure. Maybe it is mercy. Maybe it is succumbing.

Maybe the land itself has decided to take me back at last.

Or maybe it is punishment. Maybe, like the witches before me, I too will burn—punished not for what I've done, but for what I've endured.

September 6, 2025.—I sit now with pen and paper, watching as the smoke fills the sky.

Upstairs, the bat—the last mourner—rustles once more in the rafters. Soon the land that bore me, the land that cursed me, will erase me.

Let it.

But let these words remain, carried in the ashes on the wind, buried deep in the earth. If these pages survive the fire, let them be a warning—or a memory.

Once, I was Adeline Harrow, the last ghost of Harrow's End.

Before that, I was human. I loved. I lost.

I was Mina. Marked, but never quite saved.

Let them think the evil ended with him. It didn't.

It endured.

And still, I remain.

Lindy Ryan is an award-winning author, anthologist, and short-film director whose books and anthologies have received starred reviews from *Publishers Weekly*, *Booklist*, and *Library Journal*. Her work has been adapted for screen, and she was named a *Publishers Weekly* Star Watch Honoree in 2020 and one of horror's most masterful anthology curators in 2022. Ryan is the author-in-residence at *Rue Morgue*, a columnist at *BookTrib*, and the founder of Black Spot Books. She teaches at Rutgers University, mentors in WCSU's MFA program, and serves on the Board of the Brothers Grimm Society of North America.

A Mina for all Seasons
By Gwendolyn Kiste

It's long past midnight when Mina closes her eyes, and he's waiting there in the darkness. The scent of his skin like smoke and brandy, his words smoother than velvet.

And that gnarled hand of his, resting around her throat.

"Let me see to your comfort, dear Mina," he says, and her heart twists in her chest.

"Go away," she whispers, but she already knows he won't listen.

"I dreamt of him again last night."

It's morning now, and Mina is sitting up in her four-poster bed, her eyes rimmed red, the chenille bedspread in a tight tangle around her body.

Her husband Jonathan stares back at her, worry creasing his brow, and the world holds still for a long moment. The baby fusses in the next room. The radiator rattles impatiently.

"It's over, my love," Jonathan says at last, and leans across the mattress, kissing Mina's forehead. As if that's an answer.

She forces a smile, even though she knows the truth. It will never be over. Not for Mina. In the gloom, he'll be waiting for her.

In a way, she wonders if he's always been waiting.

She won't speak his name aloud. Neither will her husband. They pretend it never happened. Not the blood or the bite or the chase through the mountains.

But that's where things get hazy. She and Jonathan remember it being the nearby mountain range. The Rocky Mountains. Only that doesn't feel right. A word keeps sticking in Mina's throat like a glob of glue.

The Carpathians.

She looks them up in the encyclopedia. They're in Romania. Mina's never been to Romania. In fact, she's never been outside of America. She was born and bred here, as authentic as apple pie and Fourth of July.

That's what she tells herself. But in the dark, she can remember another life.

A perilous cliff in a place called Whitby. A real estate deal for Carfax Abbey. A castle whose namesake still haunts her dreams.

Mina wasn't always here in this home, in this country, but she's always been running from him. She has a feeling they've done this many times before in many different lives.

Through the wall, Mina hears the baby cooing, and she slips into the nursery, cradling her son.

"It's all okay," she whispers to him, but she doesn't believe a word of it.

Mina told Jonathan about it once. Her suspicion about their predicament, the way they're trapped in a cycle of a monster's making.

"How often do you think it keeps happening?" he asked, his lips pursed, his eyes gone gray.

She only shook her head. "Once a century, perhaps. Maybe more, maybe less."

He nodded, and part of her knew he believed her. She also knew there was nothing either of them could do. That's probably why they've never spoken of it again. It's easier that way.

In the afternoon, Mina folds the laundry upstairs on the four-poster bed.

With the clock ticking nervously on the wall, she closes her eyes and floats back in time, half-convinced it's nearing the turn of the century. The twentieth century. 1890 to be exact. But when she looks again, one glance at the calendar above her nightstand tells her that isn't right.

It's the middle of December in 1959. The last month of the last year in the decade. The world's on the cusp of change, the ground like quicksand beneath her. Mina doesn't know who she is, where she is.

She doesn't remember much of the lives that came before, but she remembers enough. There are certain things that always happen to her.

Jonathan abandons her for work, an opportunity that's meant to change their lives. (It lives up to that promise, no doubt about it.) Soon, a stranger arrives in darkness, with a thrall that draws Mina in. Then there's a chase through the mountains, and a bowie knife through a heart, and a happily ever after that tastes remarkably of bitterness and regret.

And she always loses Lucy, her one confidant. Her one true friend. That's the worst part. The hardest part.

Those are the rules. Mina doesn't know why.

In every iteration of herself, she's known Lucy all her life. But this version, this current life, is the one she remembers best. The Lucy with pin curls and a victory red smile. As girls, they volunteered together at the local canteen stop, serving soldiers hot meals at the train station on their way to deployment. It was the same train Mina and Jonathan would take a few years later after the second World War was over but their own war had only just begun.

By the time they boarded the train through the Rockies, Lucy was already long gone, dead and buried twice, her body burned to cinders. Mina never even got to say goodbye.

When they caught up with the monster, it wasn't quite a castle. Just a Beaux-Arts mansion of sorts, newfangled in all the worst ways. Clean lines and clean corners. But there was still darkness lurking in the rafters and cobwebs in places you would never expect. Decay follows him, whether he likes it or not.

They heard last month that his house, abandoned and unclaimed, had finally been condemned. *Bat infestation* was the official reason.

"We can't run the risk of a rabies outbreak," the locals said, and that made Mina laugh until she cried. Then she laughed a little more.

Mina fixes pot roast for dinner. Jonathan likes pot roast, and so does she. It's a solid dish, a normal kind of meal for a normal kind of family. And that's all Mina wants: something normal. Something safe.

In the living room, the television is on, staticky commercials humming in the background, as the baby naps in his crib.

While the roast is in the oven, Mina wanders in and out of the room, checking on little Quincey. He's such a placid baby, such a happy one. She's grateful he doesn't know anything about their past. She promises herself that he'll never find out.

With her hands folded in front of her, Mina's ready to return to the kitchen, the apron strings tied too tight around her waist, when she glances once more at the television screen. That's when she sees it: Lucy's face staring back at her.

"It's not too late, Mina," her best friend says with that voice like the sweetest windchime.

All the breath exits Mina's chest. This can't be real. This can't be happening right now.

She blinks once, twice, and when she looks again, Lucy is gone, a silly commercial for Lucky Strike cigarettes flashing on the screen.

The pot roast burns in the oven, the edges as black as ash. But when Jonathan arrives home, he never complains. He simply devours every bite.

"What are you thinking about?" he asks her as they lounge together on the Dunbar sofa after dinner.

Mina bites her bottom lip. "How I wish I remembered nothing at all."

The baby babbles on the blood-red carpet, but Mina isn't looking at him. She's gazing out the picture window instead, counting the minutes until sundown.

It's three in the morning, and Mina still isn't asleep. She doesn't want to close her eyes. She doesn't want to meet him again.

Next to her, Jonathan snores plaintively. He can doze through anything, and she envies him for it. Even the baby sleeps through the night now. Mina's the only one in the house who never seems to rest.

With the minutes disintegrating around her, she can keep her eyes open no longer, the world slipping away. And in the darkness, he's waiting right where she left him.

"Would you like to see what comes next?" he asks, his hand wrapped around her throat again, and before she can answer— before she can tell him no—he's already revealing it to her. A future as bleak as winter's midnight.

One by one, Mina and her little group will depart this life, starting with the doctor that led the charge. From miles away, she can see Van Helsing, a rattle in his chest, eternity in his eyes. Then Jack and Arthur will follow along with Jonathan, leaving Mina for last. Leaving Mina alone.

But even once they're gone, it almost doesn't matter. Decades from now, they'll return from the dead, reincarnated in a new world, and they'll do it all again.

This will never end. He is Death, and she is the maiden, and in his embrace, she'll always be the girl with scars on her neck and scars on her heart. Unless she can figure out another way.

Unless she can end this cycle.

The next morning, Mina burns the toast and overcooks the eggs. Jonathan doesn't complain. Jonathan never complains.

Night after night, the monster intrudes upon her dreams, revealing himself. Revealing their past. Mina meets every version of herself that came before.

A maiden in a thatch-roofed cottage during the Black Death.

A woman with a heavy heart hiding from the Inquisition.

A wide-eyed peasant in the midst of the French Revolution.

When he can, he chooses a time of pestilence or revolt, an era where he can easily hide his bloody exploits. But this time around, he didn't choose very wisely. There's a Cold War afoot, but otherwise, this is America, and you're supposed to feel safe and settled. You're supposed to feel thankful.

Mina only wishes she did.

It's three days before Christmas when there's a call late in the evening. Jonathan answers, his voice no more than a murmur. Mina lingers in the living room, eavesdropping the best she can, all the while hearing nothing at all.

At last, he hangs up the phone and returns to her, his skin gone ashen. "The doctor isn't doing well," he says. "We should pay him a visit before it's too late."

Too late for what? Mina almost asks. It's not as if they'll ever be rid of each other, not really. They'll catch each other in the next life, whether they like it or not.

But Mina doesn't argue. Instead, she bundles up the baby, and together, they drive an hour upstate to bid Van Helsing farewell.

His home looks exactly as Mina always imagined it, the curtains drawn, expensive antiques in every room, a map in the study with pins pricked into it. She wonders if all those spots mark the monsters he's dispatched.

But there will be no more hunting for him now. Van Helsing's resting upstairs in bed, his body frail and thin. "Thank you for coming, my friends," he says, and Jonathan kneels next to him, tears already blurring his eyes.

Mina, however, remains in the doorway, hardly looking up. Here's a truth she never speaks aloud: part of her blames him a little for Lucy's death.

If only he'd watched over her closer.

If only he'd kept the doors latched tighter.

If only they hadn't put their trust in a man with his own agenda, a man with his own vendettas.

If only if only if only.

But she won't think of any of that now. It's time to play the part of the good wife, the good mother, the good and grateful survivor.

Van Helsing's family drifts in and out of the room, grief sinking into them like poison. Jonathan follows them toward the hallway, all of them whispering, arranging for the inevitable. That leaves her and the baby alone with the doctor.

Mina leans closer to the bed. "I still see him."

Van Helsing squints at her, the light fading in his face. "Where?"

"In my dreams."

The old man nods, his lips pursed, as if he already knew the answer. "That's because you bear the mark of the vampire." He nods at the heart-shaped scar on her throat. "Those are the rules, dear Mina."

"Whose rules?" she asks, but the doctor has already closed his eyes for the last time. Or at least the last time in this lifetime.

Mina drives them home, Jonathan sobbing softly in the passenger seat. But with her hands steady on the wheel, she doesn't shed a single tear. Instead, she keeps her gaze on the road ahead, Van Helsing's voice still echoing in her mind.

Those are the rules, dear Mina.

The rules of men. Not her rules. Never her rules.

Christmas comes and goes, a somber affair this time around. The funeral is held at dusk, and there are familiar faces there, Arthur and Jack arriving together. They look older somehow, even though it's been less than a year since she's seen them.

After the services, Mina goes walking with the two of them while Jonathan takes the baby to the Studebaker.

"Do you ever think of it?" she asks. "Of what we had to do in those mountains?"

"Sometimes," Arthur says. "But you shouldn't bother yourself with it, lovely Mina."

"Certainly not." Jack smiles at her. "You've got that strapping young boy to worry about."

Is that all I am now? she wants to ask. *A matriarch, a mother, a madwoman?*

Because that's what it feels like: that she's going mad. That she'll never escape herself.

She'll never escape the past.

The days slip away from her, like coffin dirt between her fingers. She sees Lucy everywhere she looks. She sees the brides as well. And if she's not careful, if she steps into the shadows at the grocery store or goes walking in the downtown square after sunset, she sees him as well.

Tonight, Mina reclines in bed next to Jonathan, and she doesn't fight sleep. With her arms rested over her chest, she closes her eyes and lets the darkness wash over her.

As always, he's already waiting. "Enter freely and of your own will," he whispers.

But Mina only smiles. "I will enter nowhere at all," she says.

She bears the mark of the vampire. That means she bears some of his strength as well. He can fill her mind with his memories. She can also fill his mind with hers.

He reaches out to take her by the throat, but she beats him to it, her fingers wrapped tight around his neck. Mina remembers everything—it's her blessing and her curse. But she can use that to her advantage. All the versions of Mina pass through her mind at once, and she pours them into him, centuries of grief and gore unfurling from her.

Fear flashes in his face, because he wasn't counting on this. They never count on Mina, never see the steely resolve in her eyes. That's why he's got no defenses against her. He crumples in her hand like discarded paper, smaller and smaller until he's nothing at all. In this place, in this nightmare, her memories are better than a bowie knife to the heart.

Once he's vanished, she steps back, an ache still living in her chest. This isn't the end, and she knows it. But maybe that isn't all bad. There will be another chance, and when it arrives, she won't forget a thing. She and Lucy will open their eyes in a new life, and they'll be ready for it. They won't follow anyone's rules but their own. After all, the world is on the cusp of change, and Mina is determined to change with it. The next time she meets Dracula, everything will be different.

The next time will belong to her.

Mina descends into a dreamless sleep. She'll never dream again. Unless of course she wants to.

It's New Year's Day, a fresh January, a fresh decade, and Mina awakens alone in her four-poster bed.

Jonathan is already downstairs with baby Quincey, the two of them playing with a train set beneath the holiday tree. Her husband glances up when she walks into the room, his face brightening.

"I figured we'd just let you sleep," he says.

She nestles on the floor beside them, the three of them together. The morning light is pouring in through the picture window, and her eyes are wide open now.

She can't change what came before. It's far too late for that now. But she can change tomorrow. She can remake every lifetime they'll ever get from here.

And she'll start with this one. She can become more than the woman who survived a monster. She can become whatever she wants, the future brimming in her like a promise.

"To a new year," she says with a smile, and in this moment, the darkness feels a thousand miles away.

Gwendolyn Kiste is the four-time Bram Stoker Award-winning author of *The Rust Maidens, Reluctant Immortals, Boneset & Feathers, Pretty Marys All in a Row*, and *The Haunting of Velkwood*. Her short fiction and nonfiction have appeared in outlets including Lit Hub, Nightmare, Best American Science Fiction and Fantasy, CrimeReads, Titan Books, The Lineup, and The Dark. She's a Lambda Literary Award winner, and her fiction has also received the This Is Horror Award for Novel of the Year as well as nominations for the Shirley Jackson, Premios Kelvin, Ignotus, and Dragon Awards. Originally from Ohio, she now resides on an abandoned horse farm outside of Pittsburgh with her husband, their excitable calico cat, and not nearly enough ghosts. Find her online at gwendolynkiste.com

Whoever Fights Monsters
By Cynthia Ward

"Whoever fights monsters should see to it that he does not
himself become a monster."
—Friedrich Nietzsche, *Beyond Good and Evil:
Prelude to a Philosophy of the Future*

London, 1891

He's back.

So I find myself in the East-End, a place where
once I would never have ventured, nor imagined I should have
reason to.

They assured me he was dead—the true death—and would
never return.

But I felt him during my confinement.

I draw near Whitechapel at midnight. Few are abroad. The
pea-soup fog for once has cleared, and no winter storm portends.
The air is cutting as glass shards, though the cold no longer
bothers me so much as once it did. The scents of poverty are
sharp as vinegar, though once I would have found them muted by
the chill. Gas lamps are few here, but the stars are bright, the

moon full. I am grateful for these celestial lights, though I need them not nearly so much as once I did.

They told me—the ones who slew him—that the bond between us was broken.

But I feel him again.

I feel every time he kills.

A newspaper blows by on a knife-edge wind, yellow with the passage of days, the headline briefly visible: ANOTHER WHITECHAPEL HORROR. 'JACK THE RIPPER' AGAIN.

The newspapers have it wrong.

The one who has returned does not wish it known. Save for the night he was nearly discovered, he has hidden the bodies of the women he takes. As further protection, he obscures his true activity by knife mutilation of their necks. He makes it seem that someone else commits the murders.

But I know he has returned. Since my confinement, I feel him all the time.

I would do anything—

A man jostles me; a poor man, ragged and smelling of gin, a German immigrant by the features of him, and the hue where his skin is not smirched by soot. His eyes gleam with desperation as he reaches for me. His gaze is all for my clothes, for the appearance of the class into which I was born, and from which I am slipping.

Quickly as an adder, I strike. My empty palm is firm as a hammer as its heel meets the German's temple. He sprawls at the verge of Mitre Square. My blow was restrained. The man is only unconscious.

He was never a threat to me, or to mine.

The one who threatens all is starving. He cannot feed freely. He cannot strike every night, lest his return be known. Distracted by his thirst, he does not feel me. I must act before he sates himself enough that he can sense me, and realize what he did to me. What he created.

I approach the entrance of Church Passage, which is feebly lit by the flickers of the strong-smelling gas lamp on the wall above. Within, the passageway is black as Erebus. Its mouth exhales the odors of rotting garbage and worse. From its depths, a brief rustle issues, and is only more frightening for its faintness. Everything presses me to turn and flee.

I take a step into Church Passage.

I would do anything—

I see him, suddenly. My widening pupils find the deeper shadow within the darkness. His back to me, he approaches the place where the passageway walls draw close.

Once, I'd have seen only depthless blackness. Now, my eyes might be an owl's. He changed me in ways I could never have imagined, when he came to me in the night.

I feel him all the time.

I feel that he hunts; and now that I am close to him, I find myself seeing through his eyes. I see the woman he approaches. I see the heavy powder that covers her pinched face, and the pinned locks that spill too much of her fair hair to be proper. I see that her gaudy blue silk skirt is partially tucked up, to make a scandalous display of her petticoats. And I suppress the dangerous impulse to cry out or draw breath in shock, as I examine her face more closely, and realize this unfortunate woman cannot be more than fifteen years old.

Unaware that I am near, she turns her false smile to him and twitches her soiled petticoats. Her lips move, and I hear her East-End accent. "Fancy a bit of it, do you, sir?"

In the girl, I fear I witness my own fate; but I shall never let it be the fate of the one who is mine.

I feel him as I see what he sees. I feel him at every moment, waking and sleeping. I feel what he feels as my left hand seizes his shoulder and pulls him about.

I see his face, gaunt and ravaged with hunger, and as deathly pale as it was on the night I saw him slain. I see his teeth, parted and keen. I feel his surprise and rage and, as he realizes whom he looks upon, his recognition and abruptly increased craving. Then my body shakes and my teeth clench as I feel the pain of my stake driving deep into his heart, then the agony of my hands tearing the head from his shoulders.

Then I feel him no longer.

The girl stares, eyes widening, hands rising to her mouth. She is terribly young, but I know she must be hardened by her life. Yet at the damage I inflict, and the spill of his colorless thin blood, she screams.

"Go," I say; no more. Even if she knew of him—recognized the name of him, if I uttered it—how could she believe the truth? How could she believe that one who has done what she has just witnessed, showing a strength no longer quite human, would do her no harm? How could she believe I am anything but another monster? How could she believe, given her lot, that anyone approaching her by night is anything but a monster?

I needn't speak again. She flees.

I kneel beside the body. I know not how to accomplish it. But I must make sure he does not rise again—

"Mrs. Harker." The voice is soft and male and cultured. It is also entirely unfamiliar.

I am standing again. I changed that night, though I did not die, or become other than human. Yet my speed is other than human as I raise the bloody stake like a sword.

I face forwards—the direction from which the voice has issued—and say, "Stand forth, whoever you are."

"Or should I address you as 'Miss Murray'?" The owner of the cultured voice reveals himself, stepping from the shelter of a doorway, yards ahead.

I point my stake towards his chest, and he raises his hands to show empty palms. His hands are huge. His every movement is ponderous. I cannot determine whether his slowness arises from a distaste for exertion, or the layers of time that may slow a man in middle years, or the hindrance of remarkable size. The man is enormous, both in height and in girth. I know better than to assume he must be weakened by his weight; a man so large needs strength to move. Too, the massive breadth of his shoulders, and the clear lines of his upraised arms against their sleeves, suggest a vigour otherwise disguised by his tailoring.

However robust he might be, he has neither strength enough nor speed enough to stop me, should I choose to close the distance between us, and strike. But I am wary; he might have a hidden pistol, close to hand, and an accurate shot I would neither outpace nor survive. Yet I do not fear the man, as I would have, before I changed.

I speak. "Who are you?"

I do not ask the other question—how does the enormous man know who I am—and who I was?

Jonathan was unable to consummate the marriage. His experiences in that distant land—that gruesome castle—scarred him. When he understood that I was in a delicate condition, he knew it wasn't his.

Jonathan loved me. But expecting him to stay, when he realized all that had been done to me, was too much to ask of any man.

The enormous stranger takes his time in responding to my question. He studies me, seeming undisturbed by the stake I hold, and the head and body sundered by my hands. At length, he doffs his top hat and sweeps a bow to me.

Straightening, he says, "Your adventure tonight shall not haunt you." He gestures with his empty hand at the headless body. "We shall ensure he comes back no more."

"You haven't answered my question," I say. "Who are you? And why should you assist me?"

"In truth," the enormous man says, "it is not merely to assist you, Miss Murray, that we shall see to it the monster does not return. But this—" he indicates the headless body "—is not the only one such who hunts the night." He hesitates, with a delicacy carefully measured. "I should not ask this of you. A woman in your situation does not generally work."

I worked once. But it is not only her skills that qualify a woman for honourable employment. Unmarried girls are hired. Not women who are no longer married, yet are not widowed.

Some weeks ago, an Irish writer contacted me, saying he would like to read my journals, our letters, and tell the story, changing certain facts, in exchange for payment. It was a handsome sum, in light of all considerations, including the reality that he could write his tale without recourse to a single fact I might provide. And, I suspect, he will play very freely with the facts, and end things far more happily than the grim story I revealed to him. Yes, a very handsome sum, all told. But not enough to survive on for very long, when there are two mouths to feed.

The enormous man stands silently, holding his hat, awaiting my reply with the patience of stone.

His eyes are set deep in shadowed sockets, beneath the high sweep of his brow. Once, the sockets would have been opaque as coal to my eyes. Now, I can see his eyes are grey and sharp and unyielding as a sword-blade. Once, such eyes would have terrified me. Now, my gaze crosses his with the steadiness of a sword-master's steel.

"A woman in _my_ situation has no choice but to take up work," I tell him. "I accept."

He seems not entirely surprised by my reply, but he says, "You don't know what the position involves—"

"If it does not involve lifting my skirts, then I am ahead."

The enormous man bows his head a moment, then meets my level gaze again. Once, I should never have looked at a man so boldly, as did my closest friend, Lucy, before she changed, and was therefore destroyed. I too changed in many ways, on that night ten months ago; and that night wrought further changes, across the months. My changes are very different from those that made Lucy's destruction inevitable. The greatest of my changes forbids me to do myself harm; and it forbids me to let myself, or mine, come to harm at another's hand.

"The position is honourable, and more than adequately compensated. But it is dangerous," the enormous man tells me. "It involves secret service to Her Majesty, and the slaying of monsters—"

"What is that," I say sharply, "to what I have already experienced?"

Heavily, he inclines his head.

A thought intrudes—a sudden realization. I have never met him, but I know who this man is. "You're the consulting detective's brother—"

"Please," he says. "Call me M."

"Your offer is acceptable, M." I say. "Now, I must be going."

"Of course." He does not offer to escort me. If I cannot arrive home safely, I am unworthy of his offer. "We shall speak again soon."

He bows to me, but does not leave.

I understand. He will remain, to see to the final disposal of the body and head. I am dismissed.

I understand something else: that he understands what drives a woman in my situation.

But there is something he does not know. I have taken great care that no one should know aught about my daughter, beyond the fact that I have borne one. And Jonathan and I have both taken care that she is believed by all to be his. Jonathan believes that we both care only to protect the child's honour, and his, and mine.

Jonathan does not understand that the honour of a woman of my birth is a luxury I can no longer afford.

I am home again, safely, and more swiftly than many a carriage would have traveled. And, home again, I find my daughter crying in hunger. I raise her to my breast.

The pain is sharp. A trickle spills, a mingling of two fluids, one white as new-fallen snow, the other crimson as spilled pomegranate. I do not care about the pain, or how she draws sustenance, or how I must make a living to keep her alive and well.

I have only one care—one concern—in all the world.

I would do anything—anything—to keep my daughter safe.

Whoever Fights Monsters originally appeared in the 2014 anthology *Athena's Daughters*, edited by Jean Rabe.

Cynthia Ward has sold stories to *Analog, Asimov's, Nightmare, ReacTor/Tor.com* (with Nisi Shawl), *Weird Tales, Worlds of If*, and elsewhere. She's the editor of *Lost Trails: Forgotten Tales of the Weird West Volumes 1-2* (WolfSinger Publications) and a coeditor of *Weird Trails* (Sam Teddy Publishing). With Nisi Shawl, Cynthia co-created the Locus Award-winning Writing the Other. Her most recent novel is *The Adventure of the Golden Woman* (Aqueduct Press).

Chagrin du Vampire
By James S. Dorr

It was family that hurt most.
She'd borrowed her late mother's nationality
changing her name from Mina to Guillemette
after she realized Van Helsing was wrong,
that her fate was her fate—
vampire blood coursed her veins.
She'd explained to her husband
one late winter night
why she had to leave London
for his sake as well as hers,
hoping he'd understand.
At least he knew her.
Others, though, she realized
would persecute her
so, grieving, she started
a new life in France.
She wore black, as widows might,
walking by day only heavily veiled.
She cultivated, in time,
a sort of Gallic indifference
to matters of soul—
she did what she had to
but never in malice,
just to survive.
But what struck through her heart
was an evening in autumn, 1916
when she, in guise of a nurse,
helping tend wounded brought back from
the Somme

saw her own son, broken—
he died in her arms never knowing who she was—
and understood, for the first time, what it meant
to be all but immortal.

Chagrin du Vampire originally appeared in Issue 33.4 of *Star*Line*, Autumn 2010.

James Dorr's *Avoid Seeing a Mouse and Other Tales of the Real and Surreal* is a January 2024 release from Alien Buddha Press, while other books include *The Tears of Isis,* a 2013 Bram Stoker Award® nominee for Fiction Collection; *Tombs: A Chronicle of Latter-Day Times of Earth*; and his all-poetry *Vamps (A Retrospective)*. Specializing in dark fantasy/horror with forays into mystery and science fiction, Dorr has been a technical writer, an editor on a regional magazine, a full time non-fiction freelancer, and a semi-professional musician. He currently harbors a Goth cat named Triana, and counts among his major influences Ray Bradbury, Edgar Allan Poe, Allen Ginsberg, and Bertolt Brecht.